BEFORE THE LAST GOODBYE

SIERRA ZINKE

PLAYLIST

Here is the playlist that inspired Before the Last Goodbye!

I Ain't Comin' Back | Morgan Wallen & Post Malone

Give Heavan Some Hell | HARDY

How Do I Say Goodbye | Dean Lewis

Tough People | Drew Baldridge

Happen to Me | Russell Dickerson

High Road | Koe Wetzel & Jessie Murph

To Love Someone | Benson Boone

We Danced | Brad Paisley

Traveling Soldier | The Chicks

Killin' Me | Parker McCollum

Content Warning

- Drug and Alcohol Addiction

- Foster Care Memories

- Abandonment by Parents

- Accident and Death (on page)

- Trauma

- Sexually Explicit Scenes

Warning to readers:

There are multiple time jumps in this book as it happens over 10 years. If you feel like you time-traveled, well, you probably did.

1

T he bar is filled with smoke, permeated by the sour smell of cologne, spilled beer, and sweat from the large number of people packed together. I was in my usual spot at the front to the left of the door while Jeremiah and Elliot stood one to the right and one directly at the door, our arms folded, lips painted into thin lines. We watch as rejections happen, fake IDs are broken, and arguments began throughout the night until the sound of shouting, tables sliding across the wooden floor, and the thud of skin-on-skin contact crack through the air.

This fight has gone on too long, and it's time to intervene. Giving a curt nod to Jeremiah, we both step onto the floor. He holds one man by the shoulders and pulls him away so I can slide in the middle to begin moving the other guy away in the opposite direction.

Thwack.

The entire bar goes silent, the DJ cuts the music as I lift my hand to the corner of my mouth, tasting the metallic copper of blood in my mouth and sliding down my chin.

This asshole actually punched me in the face.

The fist flying into my face for the third time this weekend has the anger rising from within, yet again. The never-ending pit is taking hold of my body, begging to be let out, to finally put these drunken idiots in their place. *What am I doing here?*

Not realizing his mistake in his drunken stupor, he winds up for another swing before I grab his wrist, twisting his arm behind his back, and pushing him up against the wall, ensuring safety before walking through the crowd, where I can finally deposit his ass on the sidewalk.

Elliot opens the door, and I'm smacked with the thick, unmoving air that feels like something has covered me in a layer of sweat.

I shove the idiot through the doorway and out onto the sidewalk when he slurs, "I didn't, it wasn't me, he started it..."

"You swung at the wrong guy tonight, buddy, you're done. Go home and don't come back," I say, clapping him on the shoulder before turning around to see Elliot and Jeremiah standing there, smirking.

I swear, these guys like watching me boil.

Elliot brings his hand up to his chin. "You got a little something."

"Shut up, asshole. You could've helped," I reply, wiping some blood on my black T-shirt before going inside. I'm thankful there's only another hour until closing.

Part of me hoped the humidity in the air would break by the time we walked out of the bar around 5 a.m., so we aren't instantly wrapped in a wet blanket, but nonetheless, the thick air wraps around us, as the fog dances through the streets. Jeremiah, Elliot, and I are going our separate ways only to reconvene the next night for another night of this bullshit.

It's been four years since graduating from high school, aging out of the system, and ultimately finding myself homeless before Antonio, the owner of this fine dive bar, gave me the opportunity to be a bouncer.

"Look at this kid," he calls to the guy standing behind him, looking down at me where I'm sitting on the sidewalk against the brick exterior of the bar. "He's big and strong," he continues as the guy rounds the alley-

way corner. I later learned it was Elliot, his right-hand man and head of security, although I'm not entirely convinced Elliot isn't responsible for the security of a lot more than just the bar. "You are strong, kid, aren't you?" he asks, looking at me.

I nod, unsure of what exactly to say.

"Come on, let's get you inside." Antonio reaches out his hand, helping me off the ground and leading me into the bar. We chat briefly about my life, and Elliot offers a room to rent in his house if I work on his security team.

I stayed there for a year and a half, until I had enough saved and was working enough hours to rent my own apartment. It's farther away from the bar in a crappy part of town, and in less-than-ideal shape, but it is mine.

I continue walking through the fog along the sidewalk back to my ratty apartment, boots damp from the dewy, wet sidewalk, sweat dripping down the nape of my neck.

Once home, looking in the bathroom mirror, I almost recoil at my reflection.

I look exhausted, every line on my face etched deep, my normally tan skin casting a paler undertone. My eyes sagged with heavy lids. And then there's my lip, split along the side, the edges darkened from the light crust of where the blood was. The side of my face is puffy, swollen, and tender from where the punch landed. This appearance gives the impression of a burdened man, carrying not just a fight, but constant fatigue of too many nights like this.

Why am I doing this?

I look like a man carrying the weight of a war zone.

And then came reality, hitting me like a ton of bricks; *life is not a war zone, and I can't keep wasting my time here.*

But what else can I do? Where will I go?

I don't really have much besides my clothes and my phone. My apartment was furnished when I moved in, and I spend as little time here as possible. Stepping into the cool stream of the shower, hoping to wipe away the sticky, humid sweat and blood from work, I begin creating a list of things I'm good at.

1. Fighting

2. Stopping fights

3. Manual labor (lifting, moving, etc.)

The list isn't long, but there is one thing that has been said to me over and over throughout my life that I just can't get out of my head.

Why don't you put your size and anger to good use? Join the military.

First, one of the foster families when they decided we weren't a great fit, and then my guidance counselor in school. Even the army guy who came to the school often tried to get me to enlist. He was actually one of my favorite people, but at the time I was too angry at the world to listen to anyone.

God, what was his name?

Gunter? Gilbert?

Gibson. Commander Gibson.

I scroll through my phone and find Commander Gibson's contact, where I hover over it for what feels like an eternity. My inner monologue is spiraling between reaching out and not reaching out.

Would he even remember me? Probably not. He must see many kids at all the schools he attends.

But he did tell me to reach out if I ever changed my mind. But it's been almost four years. Have I changed my mind?

I hover over his contact a second longer, like a teenager who just had their heart broken and wants to reach out but doesn't want to seem desperate. I'm a desperate teenager, at twenty-two years old. The lost one, longing for an old friend to help me make a decision.

My eyelids become heavier, and I decide this can wait, so I pull the curtain closed to keep the rising sun out. I need sleep—and a lot of it. But before I drift away, I know one thing for certain...when I wake up, I'm marching my ass straight to the recruiter's office and getting all the information I can on the army.

It's time for a change.

2

The city bus almost appears to be wobbling down the road in slow motion this morning as I lean against the cool window with nothing but a small backpack, my first-generation phone, and the new boots, which I realize was probably one of the easiest decisions I have ever made. *New shoes.* I can't even remember the last time I bought a new pair of shoes. Especially after telling Antonio and Elliot, who both clapped me on the back and told me they were proud of me.

Leaving my ratty month-to-month one-bedroom apartment was probably the second easiest decision, considering the neighborhood is only getting worse, and the apartment above me flooded last week.

It'll take four buses and a taxi to get from New Orleans to Oklahoma City, and then an entire other mode of transportation to get to the base, but I can figure that out when I get there. The recruiter said someone from the base would be at the bus station to pick me up, but didn't elaborate on who that would be or how I would find them.

I guess this is the first test of the army, right? Find the stranger responsible for getting you from point A to point B and not lose your shit in the process.

Fortunately for me, I have lived my entire life by the seat of my pants, going through whatever is thrown at me.

After the last week at the bar, I'll do anything possible to leave Louisiana and never look back, and if the fastest track to doing that is joining the army, then sign me up...yesterday. It's not like anything is waiting for me here anyway.

We drive over a large bump, causing everyone and their belongings to shift and bounce around the bus; some people shriek, while others make trills and gasps as they are jostled in their seats. You would think that for a major transportation line and highway, we would have a smoother ride...but let's be honest, Louisiana doesn't care about its roads.

The bus comes to a halt outside of Oklahoma City, and it takes me a minute to realize this is my life now. I am officially out of Louisiana, and there is no reason I ever have to go back. A wave of various emotions, from nervousness to excitement, flows through my body as everyone starts getting off the bus.

Sitting in the back of the bus is mostly just out of cautious habit, having a good vantage of being able to see the entire bus, plus everyone on it. But now, sitting at the back of the bus waiting, rather impatiently, the anxiety starts to grow within me.

I've left my home, everything I've ever known and worked so hard for, for a simple change.

Once I finally get off the bus and look around, I don't see anyone who resembles a member of the United States Army, but I guess it's not like they would have a big sign that says *Army Recruits Here!* I expected this to be like the movies where I get off the bus and there he is, standing and waiting, the only person I see in a crowded room. But he isn't there, at least not front and center.

Weaving through the crowd, head on a swivel, trying to find someone who can help me, the nervous feeling turns into an empty pit in my stomach. Did I go to the right place? There's a blue sign on the wall that says Oklahoma City, so I made it. But where the hell is my ride?

Anger starts to rise inside me as I question why I trusted someone would pick me up. Not anger with the guy or the recruiter, but with myself. Because if I've learned anything in my twenty-two years of life, it's that you don't rely on anyone else because they'll ultimately let you down.

"Schmidt," a deep, gruff voice calls out.

A wave of relief washes over me as I'd never mistake that voice. The voice that provides a sense of comfort, caring that I've only recently learned. *Gibson*. I turn to see the tall man with a brown mustache, bright blue eyes, and a perpetual scowl, who changed my life all those years ago.

"Commander Gibson," I say, giving him a curt nod.

"Glad you made it, kid. I was glad to hear you changed your mind."

"Me too, sir. Just needed to get out of my own way, I suppose."

"Well, I'm glad you finally figured it out. Let's finally put that strength to good use."

I can't help but smile with a sense of pride, knowing my size and strength will actually be used for good, instead of my hard-headed aggression and kicking drunken idiots to the curb.

I'm six-five, 250 pounds, built like a tight-end, and as strong as a bull. I was always on the larger side of the spectrum growing up, which led to bullying until I put my fist through a bully's nose.

The feeling of relief and satisfaction in knowing I was able to protect myself was unreal, so I started putting in more effort to work out, becoming stronger, until school wasn't the problem.

The streets were.

"Ready to head out?"

"Yes, sir."

We begin the walk through the parking lot to Commander Gibson's vehicle, but as I exit the transportation station building, I have to pause for a second to take in the sky.

I've never seen sky like this before, endless waves of light blue that make you wonder how far it truly goes. The air is dry, and everything's out in the open. Vastly different from the thick and pressed humid air in Louisiana that makes you feel like you're unable to breathe.

Climbing into the passenger seat of the all-black Ford Explorer with dark tinted windows makes me feel almost famous. Like, there'll be some kind of security or secret service waiting for us.

There isn't, *obviously*.

We ride in silence, mostly due to my distraction from the landscape out the window. There is no real direction, just a straight shot to Fort Sill with endless highway and horizon. Tall grass plains that sway in the breeze, and dry, cracking dirt that looks like it hasn't seen rain for months.

"You've been quiet. Christ, four years ago, I couldn't get you to stop talking. Everything okay?" Gibson says, breaking the silence.

"Yeah, just taking it all in," I reply, continuing to stare out the window.

"Remember back when we first met?" he asks, a slight smirk on his face.

"Oh god, what a time. I never thought I'd make it out of there," I say, rolling my eyes, drifting back into memories.

"You were the biggest sophomore I had ever seen," he says, chuckling. "And that kid, what was his name? Dylan? He was picking on you as if he were the king of the school. I actually thought you were going to kill him."

I laugh, remembering that moment. "I probably would've if you hadn't stepped in, and then would have been expelled."

"I had to pull you off him," he says, a slight condescending tone to his voice.

"Oh, I remember. I still think that pummeling him would've been worth it," I say with a shrug. I really couldn't stand him. I lean my arm against the center console of the vehicle, and the cool touch against my elbow brings me back to that day in the high school cafeteria.

We crash against the tile floor, the cold continuing to sting my already bruised elbow from where we fell, my fingers turning white from the death grip I have on the collar of his jacket.

A hand grips my shoulder tightly, but doesn't try to pull me from Dylan's still frozen body underneath me.

"You don't want to do this, son. Trust me," a calm, quiet voice says from behind me.

Turning my head slightly to see who it is, I'm shocked to see a man, probably in his thirties or forties, crouching behind me, wearing camo pants and a solid T-shirt.

"Come on, let's go talk over there," he says, placing a hand on my shoulder and squeezing.

The authority in his voice and grip makes me let go before I even realize what I'm doing. He pulls me to my feet, and then helps Dylan to his feet, asking if he's okay and dismissing him back to his lunch table when Dylan confirms he's fine. Neither of us needs this interaction to go on record; it would be our third fight this year, and the school has a strict three-strike policy.

"Robert Gibson, United States Army. Call me Gibson," he says, holding his hand out to shake.

I reach out to return the handshake and say, "Jarred with two R's, Schmidt, sir."

"Well, Jarred with two R's, let's go talk about your future."

I scoff and mumble under my breath, "What future?"

Gibson shakes his head from in front of me as we walk back to the US Army table set up along the wall of the cafeteria.

"Schmidt," I hear the voice of my nightmares call after me from the doorway.

Principal Atkins.

Fuck. Has he been there the entire time? I swear this man has it out for me.

Gibson and I stop when Principal Atkins approaches.

When he reaches us, he loudly says, "I hope I wasn't walking into another altercation, Mr. Schmidt. You know we have a strict three-strike policy, and I'd hate to see you strikeout."

"Nope, Mr. Schmidt here was just coming to discuss his future in the United States Army," Gibson says, placing an arm around my shoulder and giving it a small squeeze.

"Oh, is that right?" Principal Atkins asks, clearly suspicious.

"Yes, sir. I turn eighteen in a few weeks and want to be able to leave right after graduation," I lie.

I've never once considered joining the army. Does the army even accept people like me?

"Well, good for you, Schmidt, maybe you will actually have a future, after all," Principal Atkins says. Gibson's grip tightens on my shoulder and doesn't let go until Principal Atkins turns to walk away. "I'll leave you to it," he continues.

We continue to the table, and when we're far enough away from everyone, I ask, "Why did you do that?"

"Do what?" he asks, as if he has no idea what I am talking about.

"Lie to Principal Atkins for me."

"I didn't lie to him; I simply didn't tell the entire story. We are coming over here to talk about your future. And I think you have a bright

future in the army. Plus, he seems like a bit of a prick, and I don't like any authority figure who picks on a kid."

I snort because "picks on a kid" is an understatement. Since freshman year, Principal Atkins has found every excuse possible to suspend me or give me detention—sometimes even when I've done nothing wrong. He's upset that the group home I'm living in requires me to go to this school, since it's the only high school within the radius.

"I don't want any stray dogs starting at my school and soiling all over the place," he said during our first meeting upon my enrollment.

Unfortunately for both of us, the state ruled against it, and I started here the next day.

"You could say that," I finally reply. "Thank you, sir, for doing that."

"No need to thank me, I was you once upon a time. Do you really turn eighteen in a few weeks?"

"Yes, sir. May twenty-third."

"Call me Gibson, kid."

"Do you really think I could join the army?"

"I do. With your size and athleticism, you would probably blow through basic training and be a great asset in the field. The only thing we need to work on is that temper of yours. There is a no-violence policy—especially during basic training—and usually the consequence is worse than the reward of the act. Are you currently training?"

"Yes, I weight-train five days a week in the school gym and run on the weekends. I, uh, don't have a lot of access outside of this building," I say, feeling a little embarrassed.

"No need to be embarrassed, I've been in the system. It's a brutal place and hardens us way younger than we deserve, but you're about to age out, so let's develop a plan for your future."

The bell rings, and I instantly tighten, knowing I have exactly two minutes to get to my next class, and that I absolutely cannot be late if Atkins is already on his warpath today.

As if he can read my mind, Gibson hands me a card and says, "I'm in town for the next week, let's meet to discuss this further, you can bring your case manager if you want."

He truly does know how the system works and the ins and outs.

I am too shocked to speak, so I just nod before taking the card and heading to my next class, US Government and Ethics, where I find myself paying a little more attention than usual.

"I was shocked when I heard your name on the list of recruits," Gibson says, his voice pulling me out of the memory.

"You remember me?" I ask, surprised. I know we spent weeks talking about me joining the army at eighteen, and he had spent weeks after that mentoring me into becoming a half-functioning adult capable of contributing to society, but he was at different schools in the region all the time; he must have hundreds of potential recruits he connects with regularly.

"Truthfully, you never forget the ones who remind you of yourself."

"Aww, don't go soft on me now, Commander," I say with a chuckle. "In reality, I came to realize that I was really angry with the world at eighteen, and I wouldn't see a positive sign or connection if it smacked me in the face. I've never had someone who believed I could be something more than trouble, besides you and the owner of the bar I worked at—but to him I was just a big body, acting as a punching bag while keeping patrons safe. I never thought this could truly be channeled for good," I finish, trying to open up about why I ditched him all those years ago.

Gibson chuckles quietly before saying, "You were always the perfect match for the Army, you just had to come to the realization yourself.

"I didn't know that at the time," I say with a slight whine to my voice, knowing this always gets a laugh out of him. "But in reality, I'm grateful you gave me the time of day, you saw a kid in need and really made a difference in him."

Gibson's face reddens, and this is my favorite version of him. Gibson is a strong, independent man who completely changed the trajectory of his life through hard work and dedication, but he isn't one to accept praise or love well. Hell, he doesn't show emotion, so if I can truthfully say something meaningful to see this side of him, I always will.

"You would've found your way without me," he says, looking straight ahead at the road.

"Yeah, making minimum wage and getting punched in the face regularly," I reply.

"That is not true."

"Oh no, it absolutely is. That fight would have gotten me expelled, which would have gotten me removed from my group home, and then, with how close I was to aging out, I wouldn't have been a placement priority, and would have probably run away. *Again.* You stopping that fight completely changed the direction of my future. You let me know that I had a future, that there was something out there for me. Hell, Gibson, you met with me every other week just to make sure I had support. You believed in me when no one else did. And for that, I am eternally grateful. Even if I ignored it until now."

His face reddens again, and there is a slight crack in his voice when he speaks. *Oh god, did I say the wrong thing?* "I wasn't lying when I told you I was you once. I was in the system, you know that. But what you don't know is that I was also told that I had no future. There was nothing I would ever be good enough to do, and I was a waste of space. I know what that does to the young mind. I know the damage and the trauma that it can cause. No one believed in me until I showed them what I was made of. Everyone deserves to have someone who believes in them, through the good, the bad, and the ugly. Even you, Jarred with two r's," he finishes with a smirk and no more emotion deep in his voice.

I say nothing, knowing if I do, my voice will break the same, and I am only a short drive away from walking into the biggest adventure of my life—where weakness is not an option.

The fluttering feeling in my chest quickens as we pass the first sign for the base, and I know everything is going to be different. There will be no more running out to the bayou or finding shade under a cypress tree. There will only be the future, the desert, the brotherhood, and the feeling of home I hope to build.

I keep telling myself that it's just excitement, but truthfully, it's more than that. It has to be. The indescribable feeling of the unknown.

Off in the distance, I see hills—small at first, rolling gently over the plains, and then rapidly growing into mountains. But not like the mountains in postcards where they are all snow-capped, jagged, and dramatic. These are worn down with round edges that seem to scream "hello" to the generations of people who have traveled them.

There must be a look of surprise or awe on my face, because Commander Gibson speaks. "Even something simple can be pretty, huh? Almost breathtaking the first time."

"I've never seen anything like this before. My entire life has been in the city or the swamp. This feels almost unreal."

"Let me give you some advice, kid. Everything about your life has been unreal, and it's likely going to continue that way with the Army. But only you get to decide what you do with that. If it will be a good or bad unreal. Make those choices wisely."

"Yes, sir," I say quickly, quieter than expected.

I've never thought of my life as unreal, because it has always been just my life. But it was unreal. Unreal that my parents abandoned me. Unreal, I survived those foster families just looking for a check. Unreal I actually graduated from high school. But the most unreal thing is actually being in this car in this moment with the one person who believes in me.

Life really is how you choose to look at it and respond. And in this moment, I vow to myself to always try to look at the good.

The green Fort Sill mileage signs begin popping up more regularly. First ten miles. Then five. Then every mile. The yellow warning signs indicating to watch for military vehicles make me chuckle. I'm actually in a place where you need to watch for tanks and Humvees crossing the road.

My stomach does somersaults when I see a group of soldiers on a service road. Real people. Soldiers who survived basic training and earned their camo.

More somersaults. That could be me in ten weeks, maybe. If I can make it.

No. I will make it.

The rest of the drive is a blur until we reach the big gates and the sign that says Fort Sill. The big letters and American flag don't feel like home yet. But there's a warm and welcoming feeling knowing I'm finally here in the place I've thought about for weeks.

The training, uniform, and orders are becoming something bigger than everything I left behind.

"You made it, Jarred," Commander Gibson says, looking at my smiling face. "Welcome to your new home for the next few weeks."

My palms are sweating and I have a knot in my chest the size of a cannon. I don't want to let him down, but I can't stop smiling.

I'm here. I made it.

3

The sharp, piercing noise of the Reveille playing at zero four thirty hours every morning hits me like a freight train. I should have prepared more for the drastic change in schedule. From working all hours of the night and sleeping most of the morning, to the exact opposite is not an easy transition, one that I'm unsure I'll survive.

Sleep has never come easily to me, often lying awake at night staring at the ceiling or sneaking out of whatever temporary housing I was in, to run until my mind quieted enough that I could bury myself in the mattress and doze for a few hours. The constant spinning of my mind, questioning not only my next meal or who I'd run into that day, but my past and where my birth family was, also made it easy to take the bouncer job Antonio had offered.

But this alarm, the Reveille, as they call it, will be the actual death of me. Just as my eyelids and limbs become heavy and my mind slides into a fog, the loud sound jabs repeatedly into my skull, indicating the start of our day. On day seven, I contemplate the repercussions of staying horizontal, but the Reveille doesn't care. The sound drills into you with a constant rhythm that can't be ignored.

It's clear my old life is gone—no more late nights, no more deciding when to wake or what my day consisted of, just that damn bugle dragging me out of bed for the day I'm not sure I am ready for.

I find a seat in the cafeteria when I hear someone who decides it's a good idea to start talking shit to the people at his table, as if I'm not sitting two tables away.

"You want to say that to my face, asshole?" I slam my hands on the table and push up from the bench, patience already thinning.

"I'm surprised to see you here, I always thought you'd end up in jail. Or are you here because nobody loves you enough?" he says, returning the motion.

"What the fuck do you know?"

"Why don't you come find out?"

I've dealt with enough idiots in my bouncer days that I stand and start walking toward the table when I recognize him—Dylan. Dickweed Dylan. How the hell have we not run into each other until now? Also, what is he doing here? Most importantly, how am I going to make it the next nine weeks without killing him?

Anger rises in me, my insides boiling like that night at the bar. I make a mental note to find a way to get that in check.

Before I can really get moving, I come face-to-face with an unfamiliar face, standing firm in front of me. He places two large hands on my chest, pushing me back to my table.

"The fuck was that for?" I ask, the tunnel vision toward Dylan disappearing. I realize this is the kid whose bunk is near mine. I can't remember his name, but he's tall with brown hair and blue eyes, athletic, but definitely not a weightlifter. I would probably consider him a pretty boy if his hands weren't calloused and blistered. And not freshly calloused—old, hard callouses deep into the pads of his hands.

"Sit down and calm down, or you'll get in trouble."

I know he's right; I really can't afford to have any trouble. This is my only opportunity to make something with my life, and I can't waste it on someone who doesn't know their ass from their elbow.

There is some ruckus happening behind us, but he doesn't take his eyes off me. His look is stern, wise, as if he's been through this a million times, not for the first time like the rest of us. Clearly, this guy has been through something, something leading him to his point in his life, and I respect that. I respect the grind to get not only where we are but through it, and know we need some sense of camaraderie to do it.

But there is something about him that makes me want to know more, like, why would he help someone like me?

"Kneland, Noah," he says, reaching his hand out for a handshake.

"Schmidt, Jarred," I say, not returning his gesture.

We hear the loud command from the drill instructor indicating that breakfast is over and we're to file outside for our daily physical training. During the yellow phase of training, or the first two weeks, we spend the day in a variety of training and classes, learning the Army values and pairing them alongside the physical training and obstacle courses, which we are required to navigate both individually and as a team.

The sun isn't even fully up as we line up shoulder-to-shoulder for today's formation run. Shuffling into place, my legs feel heavy from the first few days of constant movement and little sleep, but there are no other options.

The early morning air is damp and humid, burning my lungs with every inhale as my boots thud against the pavement in unison with the other recruits. Noah and I run side-by-side, shouting in response to the drill sergeant for fear of being singled out.

Today, we're fortunate that it's primarily a classroom day, where we will have a run this morning, hours of learning morals, values and designations within the Army, and will have the opportunity for some personal time later. Personal time is code for writing letters to family and receiving any mail we may have before dinner, and one last physical training session.

We're only allowed to write letters one day a week—starting the second week. This is mostly because we're so busy or delirious with exhaustion by the end of every day. Today is the first day we're able to write our families, so everyone rushes back to their bunks when the personal time starts.

Everyone around me with their pens to paper, writing furiously to make sure all their words are there, while I sit here awkwardly staring at them with nothing in hand, is a special kind of torture.

I'm basically the awkward guy at the party who has no friends and stands off to the side alone, watching.

So I pick up a piece of paper and a pen to maybe start writing, to no one in particular. It's not like I'm going to send this damn thing anyway, but I've been to enough therapists and met with enough social workers to know that writing is the appropriate coping mechanism for the anger I'm feeling.

A bend in my bunk indicates someone has sat next to me, and pulls me out of my thoughts, only to realize that I have the pen on the paper but haven't moved it . I look up to see Kneland sitting next to me.

"Hard time finding the words?" he asks, looking at my blank paper.

"Something like that," I reply and toss both pen and paper to my side.

"I get that sometimes, want to talk about it?"

"No." Why would I want to talk about the fact that it has nothing to do with having nothing to say, but everything to do with having no one to say it to. No one to tell that I'm angry, angry that no matter what I do I can't escape my past. I can't escape the places that haunt my every dream and every moment I'm awake. Angry that I did everything, *everything*, right to get here—grades, fitness, therapy, every "yes, sir," "yes, ma'am,"—and still in a matter of seconds, one jackass from high school can completely throw it out of the window.

"My dad died when I was in high school," he says quietly, hands clasped in his lap, looking at them. "After that, I was angry. My mom fell into a deep depression and couldn't take care of my little sister, who was barely ten at the time. I was so angry at her. We lost our father, we couldn't lose her, too. It felt like she was making a choice, a choice that hurt us every time she couldn't get out of bed. Every day, she chose to let her illness take over and put her children second. Every day, she let us lose another parent. I stopped playing soccer, I lashed out, I gave up a scholarship to be there for them, afraid that every day she would stop being a parent and Bec, my sister, would have no one. Until one day, one day I told my best friend everything, and he told me I wasn't alone. That I didn't have to carry everything myself. My mom was grieving and it was something she needed to do, and it was okay I was angry—but I wasn't alone. I would never be alone, I just needed to learn when to accept support."

Fuck. He really has been through it.

But why would he just share that with a stranger? Someone he's known for barely a day. We're all buying our time and role here for the United States Army, there is no room for weakness. No room for feelings or tears.

But yet, I feel compelled to give him something, to let him in.

"You don't have to talk about it, and you can be angry for as long as you need to, but know you are not alone in this journey. And as a unit, we need to have each other's backs. So know that I have yours," Noah says quietly.

"His family was one of my foster families back in Louisiana, you can probably tell how that went," I say, trying to give him some semblance of the truth—at least part of the truth I can talk about.

He just nods, and it's such a small gesture but it feels so welcoming. Like when you walk into a coffee shop on a cold, rainy day and the air is warm, the barista smiles at you, and you just know you came to the right place. A feeling I'm not used to. The only other time I've felt this was with Commander Gibson, the only person who ever believed in me getting out of Louisiana.

***

The constant hum of the crickets and cicadas finally begin to slow as the sky changes to an orangey pink from the sunrise in the distant. It must be around zero six fifteen hours if the sun is starting to rise, and we have been on this course for at least an hour and a half. The thick, humid air has our bodies dripping in sweat as we run through this obstacle course. Kneland and I lead our squad as we see the end of the wooded area open up to the sunrise over another dreaded mud pit.

There's a sudden crack of a branch followed by a large thud, someone yelling, "shit!" and a grunt. Then, the sound of someone hitting the ground, and hitting the ground hard. Except I know that grunt anywhere...*Kneland.*

I turn to see him waving the rest of our group on, followed by the splashing sound of people hitting the mud pit.

I look to see most of our group crawling through successfully—and rather quickly—leaving a sense of pride in our team—we are really great together. But when I turn back, to Kneland, he is writhing in pain, face crinkled, eyes tightly closed, and I begin to worry.

I drop next to him, as he clutches his arm tight to his abdomen.

"Hey, you okay?" I ask cautiously, looking him over for any signs of major injuries.

"Landed. On. My. Shoulder," he says between breaths.

"Okay, come on, let's get you up and going, we have got to be close to the end and we'll get it looked at then."

Noah doesn't say anything before slowly moving to his knees and back up to his feet. There appears to be no injuries, other than his shoulder, which he is clutching close to his body as we move toward the mud pit. The rest of the group is on the other side waiting for us to come through so we can finish the course as a cohesive unit.

Kneland's run is slower than normal, with an uneasiness, almost like a limp but with his upper body.

We get to the mud pit and he motions for me to go first. With a splash, I begin crawling under the wire, making sure to open my ears for signs of Kneland following. At first I hear the splash and am met with some droplets of mud landing on my already mud-covered uniformed, but then I hear a groan followed by a larger splash. Turning my head back and tilting slightly, I see him face down in the mud, almost shaking.

I shimmy back to align myself next to him, mud splashing off my boots.

His face is pressed into the mud, and I can see almost a visible gap in his shoulder between the shoulder and the arm.

"What happened?"

"I can't pull myself, my shoulder is wrecked," he says, trying to move his arm up again, then failing. He looks at me with a look of sorrow before saying, "You need to keep moving, the group is waiting for you."

"Hey, no, look at me," I say, moving an arm to place my hand on the side of his arm before continuing. "We don't leaving anyone behind, remember? That includes you. You're a part of this, Kneland."

"Schmidt, I literally can't. You have to keep going."

"Then I guess we're going to crawl together," I say, ignoring his comment and placing my arm under his bad side to take some of the weight.

He just gives me a curt nod, paired with a hint of annoyance as we begin crawling side-by-side, one arm at a time through the mud pit. The mud smells pungent, like a mix of life and death, as the leaves falling decay beneath the water and dirt. We're covered head to toe, in the thick layered mud by the time we reach the end, where some of our other unit members, Gage and Ryan help pull us out.

"See, I told you we'd make it through," I say between breaths, body shaking with exhaustion.

"Yeah, thanks, man," he replies, turning toward me. "I owe you."

"Nobody is getting left behind, Kneland, even you. I've got your back always."

"Always," he says, putting his good arm out for a fist bump.

I chuckle before returning the gesture and say, "Let's finish this thing and get you looked at."

4

10 Weeks Later

The sun is shining bright in Oklahoma, and I can't help but imagine it's to mimic the excitement of this upcoming weekend. It's October in the south, so the weather is usually a hit or miss. It is typically hot, like the type of heat where you may as well wait to shower because you'll be dripping before you even get fully outside. Rain is fairly common here, but it often comes in the form of an afternoon thunderstorm or morning shower, and is not typically an all-day affair.

This week has been bittersweet in that we finalized all our tests. Noah and I passed, meaning we can move on with our military careers and have more free time. However, it also means graduation is coming up, and I can't help but wonder if I'll be the only one all alone.

I hear the patter of recruits running around the barracks, cleaning, packing, and their distant, excited chatter. Graduation's tomorrow, and people are scrambling—to clean, to find places near base for their families to stay, and everything in between.

The chaos makes me almost grateful that I have no one to show up. My family is right here, Commander Gibson and me—the only family I need.

Who would've thought that a bunch of guys cared so much about graduation?

Me.

I care about this graduation.

This graduation is *everything* to me, secretly. It's the final transition from my past.

The past of a battered kid, angry, causing trouble, who would do anything to not only survive but be seen and loved. I am leaving behind as I plow into the future as a strong man who doesn't need to be seen or loved to know I'm making a difference. I'm serving our country and showing everyone who doubted me that I can become something.

And I'm going to continue to shove it in their faces.

Noah falls into the category of people similar to me, excited for graduation but also running around like a chicken with its head cut off.

"It's crazy that in just three days our families will be here," he says from across the bunks.

"Yeah," I say. Noah may have become the closest thing to a friend I have ever had over the last ten weeks, but not close enough to truly know that I am completely alone.

"Any idea where our orders will be?" I ask, trying to hide the nerves from my voice. This is the farthest I've ever traveled, and I only went through four states, without getting off the bus in any of them.

I'm not nervous about being thrown into combat, active fire, or even the potential of dying in the line of duty. I'm nervous about flying, potentially across the world, not knowing the language, culture, or how to fit in with the other soldiers.

Hell, I don't even know how to book a plane ticket.

My hands start to sweat against my pants as the nerves to ignite my core.

"I don't, but I imagine going overseas with everything going on in our fucking insane world," Noah says, looking at me as if he is analyzing every breath I take. Noah has been the best friend I could possibly ask for, not that I know what that looks like, but he is the epitome of what I imagine a good friend would be.

He is always there, but not in the pressing, nagging way. He will just be present, listen when I'm angry, and provide advice when asked. I was having a particularly shitty day, I let Dickweed Dylan get under my skin again and was struggling to hold my anger together, when Noah asked me one of the most valuable questions I have ever heard.

"What do you need right now? Someone to listen or someone to give advice?"

I can't imagine being twenty years old and having that much wisdom and love for everyone around them. I have seen Noah not only be that person for me but everyone in our unit. BTC is challenging; it is a test of not only physical strength but also mental strength. Hell, we lost about half the people we started with during these grueling ten weeks, but our unit is the only one that remained completely intact, and that is solely due to Noah and his devotion and leadership.

"Who is this handsome man?" I hear a woman ask as she approaches Noah and me. There are two young girls with her, one matches the vague description Noah gave me of his long-distance "girlfriend," Olivia. The one he can't stop talking about. It's cute, really, how obsessed he is with her. The other has to be at least six years younger than us with a short, almost black bob perfectly styled in beach curls that fall above her shoulder to match her black denim skirt and tan shirt.

I guess she's probably his sister, the one he swears is annoying as hell, the biggest trouble maker in the town but also a complete free spirit. She won't let anyone sway her. The way she walks gives off a *no fucks* attitude, paired with the thin line her mouth is pressed into.

Does she even want to be here?

Noah elbows me on the side.

"What?"

"She's talking to you, dumbass."

Me?

I turn to look behind me, faking confusion and point to myself before saying, "Me?"

"Oh, he's funny, too," the older woman says. "Noah, you weren't joking when you mentioned how big he was. Good Lord, boy, what are they feeding you?"

"Iron," I say, uncomfortable by the interaction. Before arriving in Oklahoma, there were days I spent more time at the gym to avoid the constant gnawing at my stomach lingering after forgetting to go to the store, yet again.

"Mom, stop," Noah says before the silence gets unbearable. "Schmidty, this is my mom, Martha, my little sister, Rebecca—"

"Bec," she corrects, interrupting him and rolling her eyes all at once.

"Bec. And my amazingly, beautiful girlfriend Olivia"

"Gag," Bec interrupts again, laughing this time.

Noah glares, Olivia blushes, and Martha elbows her gently in the side. Me, I can't help but laugh along with her.

"Everyone, this is Schmidt," Noah finally says, ending the awkward introductions.

"Jarred, call me Jarred, please, Ms. Kneland," I say, sticking my hand out for a handshake.

"Oh please, boy, we hug in this family," she says, pulling me into a brief hug. My entire body tenses, not expecting it. I can't actually remember the last time someone gave me a hug.

"Jarred, when is your family arriving? I'd love to meet them, maybe we can all go to dinner after graduation," Ms. Kneland asks.

My entire world instantly crashes down around me. My stomach twists in knots and I feel nausea start to creep up my throat.

Am I about to tell a stranger about my past?

"*Mom*," Noah scolds from ahead us on the sidewalk, arm wrapped around Olivia's waist, holding her close to his side. We decided to give them a brief tour of the grounds before getting ready for dinner and graduation tomorrow.

"It's okay, Kneland," I offer in reassurance that I was okay. "I actually don't have any family coming this weekend, I aged out of the system and ended up here."

"Oh! Well then, you'll be doing everything with us! You're a part of our family now, and no one gets left behind," she responds, placing a gentle hand on my shoulder. Her touch, warm and welcoming, makes it difficult to refuse. There's no pity, nothing that indicates she's just doing this because she feels guilty or bad for me. They're just genuinely an incredibly kind group of people. When her hand leaves my shoulder, it leaves me craving more. More warmth and love that I don't recall ever experiencing from my own mother.

But I guess it's hard to exude warmth and love when you're higher than a kite and disappear for days on end.

"That's really not necessary—"

"Nonsense," she interrupts me with such a tone that I know I won't be arguing any further.

We get to dinner later that night and notice a slight shift in Noah's demeanor. He may be the master of reading me, but he's also shit at hiding his own emotions. Earlier, he was all over Olivia, laughing, sharing stories back and forth about her time in the big city, wherever that is, and his time here.

He didn't know she was coming to graduation, and I wish I could've seen his initial surprise when she arrived.

She seems to have pulled off the biggest surprise, arriving in Oklahoma to surprise him for graduation and telling him she's in love with him. Bec is right, the cuteness overload between them is gross.

Maybe this is just what love looks like?

But as we sit around the table, he isn't smiling; he's even leaving some space between them. Olivia's just as giddy as before, talking about the future, guessing where our orders are taking us. It's painstakingly obvious how much she loves Noah, and more so, how excited she is to be here.

"I did some research, and it said that they keep new graduates stateside for the first year, to get more training and experience," she says with a soft smile.

Noah tenses next to her face shifting into a scowl for all of three seconds before quickly schooling it back into a gentle returning smile.

"I'll take this one," I chime in. "We won't find out where we're going until after graduation, and you're right we will be stateside but only as we go through AIT, another form of training. We may have some time to get everything together before leaving for that destination. There's actually no guarantee we'll even be sent to the same place," I say, trying to add in a serious tone, hoping to stop the prying.

It isn't a lie. Everything is up in the air. We hope to stay with our closest recruits. We all do, but you go where you're told, no questions asked.

"Oh," she says, shoulders sagging. This place feels too fancy for such a sad conversation. This weekend is about celebrating our accomplishments, not worrying about the future. There will be plenty of time for that.

We had to travel to the city to find a dinner location that was up to Ms. Kneland's standards, which is when I learned that Noah's family lives comfortably, and I can't help but wonder what that lifestyle is like.

I know his dad had passed away when he was younger, but I couldn't picture little Ms. Kneland continuing the political campaigns and events even afterward.

The white tablecloth has a slight golden glow to it, illuminated by a single candlestick in the center of the table surrounded by small square vases carrying single rose heads in them. Ms. Kneland ordered a bottle of red wine and she, Olivia, and Noah each take a glass. I've never been in a restaurant this nice before in my life. Hell, I have never dressed this nice before and wouldn't have been able to, if it wasn't for Kneland.

Ms. Kneland smiles at me from across the table like I belong here, making my chest tighten with anxiety and nervousness. I nod along in their conversation, saying thank you and smiling when they express pride in our accomplishments. But I feel like I'm in someone else's body, like I don't belong in a place this nice. I'm in someone else's body, wearing someone else's clothes and

I need to breathe. Really breathe. Get a full breath in to let out and go back to the dirt and sweat and simple life.

"I'm going to get some air, be right back," I say, placing my napkin on the table and sliding my chair back before stepping away and un-buttoning the top button on my collar. Once outside, the cool night breeze relaxes every muscle in my body.

"I used to feel like that, too," I hear, and turn to see Ms. Kneland leaning against the wall behind me. "Like I didn't belong, wasn't meant to be a politician's wife," she continues.

"I'm sorry, ma'am, I didn't mean to offend you," I say quickly.

"Oh, stop with the ma'am, honey. You didn't offend me. I know how you feel. I grew up in a one-bedroom apartment with my mom and three siblings. The first time I came to dinner with my late husband was with him and his parents at a place like this. And I felt like I was choking in my own skin."

"It's like you read my mind," I say through a broken laugh.

"It's a pretty standard feeling. But it's important to know you deserve to be here. You achieved something great and deserve to be celebrated for it," she says, bringing me in to a gentle hug.

"Noah has told me a bit about your past. You'll always have a place in our family," she says, squeezing me tighter. The air in my lungs would be squeezed out of me if I'm not so completely taken back by her words. She's only just met me, but in the last eight hours she's made me feel more loved and accepted than ever before.

"Thank you, Ms. Kneland. It means a lot," is all I can muster up for a response.

Wrapping her arm through mine, she says, "Nonsense, it's the truth. Now, call me Martha and let's get back inside and enjoy our dinner. You boys have a big day tomorrow."

And in that moment, something changes inside me.

Because her words mean something.

This means something.

And maybe, just maybe, I'm allowed to be happy, too.

5

The high-shining sun is boiling me from the inside in this uniform, and being surrounded by all of the recruits and their families increases the heat tenfold. But as graduation comes to an end, I half expect everyone to run to cooler climates before we head to the rented space to celebrate.

But when the company is dismissed from graduation formation, most of us slowly drifted toward the admin building. There's a large bulletin board outside where they post announcements, as well as our first set of orders.

I wave to Martha, Bec, and Ollie as they make their way down the bleachers, and notice Noah's looking down, not making eye contact or waving back to his family.

I wipe my hands on the side of my pants, nerves filling me from the toes up. Weeks of running, training, and building connections, all leading to this moment where we find out where we are going next.

The brick building has a small crowd gathering around it, all of the recruits wading past one another to access one little paper.

"Move it, Harris," Dylan says, pushing his way through the front.

"I see, even after ten weeks, morals haven't been hounded into him," I hear Noah mumble under his breath. I can't help but chuckle. After that first interaction, we have pretty much steered clear of each other, and I'm grateful for it.

The group disperses one at a time, some with heads held high, others with chins lowered, nerves flaring over their next steps. Obviously, we all have preferred specialties and training, but whether or not we end up there is a different story.

Finally, it's our turn, and we approach the board togehter, Noah, standing just shorter than me, leans in close to the board and lifts his hand in the air.

"Fort Huachuca," he says quietly leaning closer to the bulletin board. "What about you, Schmidty?"

I take a step closer to the board, skimming down toward the bottom, knowing we'll be in alphabetical order. Sliding past Kneland, I cannot help the smile sliding across my face when my gaze lands on my name. *Schmidt, Jarred – 1ˢᵗ Infantry Division, Fort Huachuca.*

I know we were both heading toward intelligence but to be headed to AIT with my best friend, seems like a gift from a God I didn't know existed, but will forever be indebted to. We know that basic training is hard, but our careers are just beginning, and we have no clue what's in front of us. And being able to do it together is pure luck.

I see the exact moment Noah realizes it, too, his tanned skin bunches up at the top of his cheeks as his grin truly expands ear to ear. His blue eyes are almost sparkling in a moment of happiness I haven't seen in him since yesterday.

"No way."

"Yes, way," I say, returning the grin. "Guess you can't get rid of me yet."

We stand there, shoulder to shoulder, as if in a modified formation, as other recruits fall in around us, analyzing their fates. Some of their faces light up, matching ours, while others fall. We truly have luck on our side, heading into this next chapter together.

"Holy shit, we're going together," he exclaims, pulling me into a hug, and for the first time, I let him.

"We have a week to get to Arizona," I say after a few seconds, excitement disappearing, realizing that I have a week with nowhere to go. I wasn't ready to go straight to Arizona, but I have nowhere to stay here or in Louisiana.

Shit. I should've kept my apartment.

"You have to come to Fisher Creek with me!" Noah says with more excitement than before, it's like he just won the lottery.

Shaking my head, I reply, "I couldn't impose on your family like that."

"Bro, it's not an imposition if I invite you." His smile starts to shrink off his face, into something more like disappointment.

"But you'll be with your family...." I start.

"Don't even try that, I know my mom tried to get you out for the holidays, and since we'll be training, you have to come now. You can't disappoint Ms. Kneland," he says, giving me the grown man equivalent of puppy dog eyes.

But he's right, I could never disappoint his mom, not after the kindness she has shown me in the last two days.

"Fine. I'll think about it. Now fix your face, you look stupid," I say, giving his shoulder a little shove.

6

I 'm not expecting the airport to be busy, but I've also never flown before now. The airport in Oklahoma City is full of people of all sizes and ages, but the holidays aren't for another month, and it makes me wonder where all these people are going. What is it like to travel? To see family in other parts of the country? Smile and laugh with excitement or anticipation of what's to come?

I'm not a religious person. I never grew up going to church—even when my foster families went, they rarely brought me with them. Personally, I'd like to think it was more from fear of the public eye, as I tended to cause some trouble. But I do believe someone was out there looking out for us and driving us to where we are today. Without that hope, would I even have made it to eighteen? Probably not.

Once I pass through the bustle of the airport and make it to the gate for my plane, it's much easier to settle into the environment. Busy places have always been the actual bane of my existence because my anxiety levels heighten and I constantly feel like I have to look over my shoulder. But it's nearly impossible to be aware of every person around you when there are so many children running circles, crying, parents yelling and arguing, and happy couples excited to be traveling every direction I look.

I find a seat in the back against the wall, place my backpack at my feet, and put my headphones on. I'm finally able to take a deep breath and my heart rate is finally normalizing. God, why did I let Noah convince me this was a good idea? I'm a Southern boy, I have never been on an airplane, let alone to a place that often has snow. Hell, I have never seen snow. I've heard it's cold, wet, and beautiful when it falls, but to experience it? Along with everything else?

Noah has been one of the best friends I could have asked for. He saved my ass in basic many times, and I still struggle to wrap my head around letting someone in, someone supporting me in all aspects of life, is weird. Why would people do that?

Because not everyone is out to get you. Noah's voice fills my brain, and I just shake my head knowing he's right. In just ten weeks, basic training has given me everything I could have possibly needed outside of Louisiana: a purpose, and most importantly, a support system and family I never knew I needed.

Which is why I am suffering through this airport to spend the next week in Fisher Creek with Noah and his family, per Ms. Kneland's request. Noah had traveled home with his family, wanting to spend as much time as possible there before we head to Arizona. I hate feeling like I am imposing on anyone's time or family, so I elected to stay on base for a few days and allow them some privacy.

"We're going to begin boarding at Gate A27 in just a few moments," a voice booms overhead, startling me. There's a huge influx of people walking toward the gate, and I impulsively pull my backpack closer to me, as if someone is going to come rip it out of my hands and sprint away.

"Now boarding active military members at Gate A27," the voice booms again, and this time, I see a tall woman standing at the gate door with the microphone.

I'm active military, but why do I get to board early? Whatever. I just signed away the next four years of my life; I may as well enjoy the perks.

***

"What the fuck was that landing?" the man next to me says as we each have death grips on our seats as we bounce against the tarmac.

Bill, my seat neighbor, is convinced I will love the small town spirit and the snow. But as the gust of cold air bombards me while I walk up the jet bridge, I am doing two things:

1. Determining if Bill has lost his marbles.

2. Cursing Noah out for not warning me about this.

As I walk down the stairs to the pickup area, I see the tall, goofy face of my best friend, who's holding a piece of cardboard, and I'm instantly confused.

"Welcome to Fisher Creek, asshat."

I choke out a laugh.

"Hey, dickhead," I reply, dropping my backpack to the floor and giving him a high-five hug to pull him in. We haven't seen each other in literally twenty-four hours, and, although we've only known each other for ten weeks, it feels like an eternity. I remember exactly what life was like without Noah, and I know I never want to experience it without him.

I have to squint when we walk outside toward the car, as the sunshine is reflecting off the snow in a blinding manner. It's like being at the beach when the sun is too bright and you use your hat to block your eyes to keep your head from exploding. Except it's easily negative degrees outside, and I don't understand how it can be so bright and snowing at the same time.

"It's a two-hour drive out to Fisher Creek. Anything you want to do before we head to the country?" Noah asks, as if I would have any idea what to do in Milwaukee, Wisconsin. I don't think I even knew people actually lived in Wisconsin. I should've paid more attention in school.

"Nah, I'm good, show me the town that created Kneland," I reply, settling into the old Toyota Corolla, wondering what it is like to own a car. There's always a constant argument in my head, like the devil and angel. The devil is constantly questioning everything and everyone, and the angel is reminding me I got out, this is my life now, and I get to take control.

Driving out of the city, we turn onto this narrow two-lane road, where there's a few inches of snow piled up on either side of the highway.

"We got the first snowfall last night, almost wasn't sure I'd make it down to get you," Noah says noticing me glancing back and forth between the windshield and the side window.

"The first snowfall of the season?" I ask, having difficulty comprehending what more snow would be like piled on either side of the cleared road. The tree branches are hanging low from the weight of the snow, making me feel like I'm in that movie where the kids walk into the wardrobe and end up in this wintery wonderland.

"Yeah, we get forty-five inches each year," he answers.

"That's actually wild," I reply. It truly is beautiful, though, and the closer we get to Fisher Creek, the more mesmerized I am by the perfect decorations and string lights hanging throughout the downtown area. I hear a man on the radio singing about heartbreak, and am instantly pulled into reality.

"What the hell is this?" I ask

"What?" Noah replies.

"This music, what the hell are we listening to?" I repeat, knowing full well it's country music, but I've never actually listened to it. I can't explain the feeling I have listening to this song, the lyrics about someone seeing who a young man truly is when he couldn't see it himself. A song that sits obnoxiously too close to home for me, as I never would have made it to this point in my life if I hadn't met Commander Gibson.

Noah looks at me with a sideways glance, confused.

"Country? Are you telling me you've never heard country music before?"

"No, I haven't. I may be from the South, but you don't listen to country music on the streets of Louisiana when trying to avoid the gangs," I reply, not breaking eye contact with him. I know this makes him uncomfortable, but if he is going to be the next person in charge of our squad, then it's important to know that he handles uncomfortable situations with grace and poise.

Noah chuckles, breaking the tension, before saying, "That's fair."

When we pull into the long winding driveway of his home, I see Ms. Kneland and Rebecca standing outside on the deck, waiting for us, each with a steaming cup in their hands.

"Hi, Ms. Kneland, thank you for inviting me," I say cautiously, walking up the salt- and sand-covered stairs. Having never walked across ice or experienced cold weather in any capacity, I make extra note not to embarrass myself in front of the family that has graciously let the boy with nothing spend the holidays with them.

"Oh, honey, call me Martha," Ms. Kneland says, handing me the cup in her hand. "Where's your coat? You're going to freeze out here."

I feel the heat rise as my face reddens with embarrassment. I don't have a coat. I've never had a coat, but really there has never been a need for one in Louisiana.

"I have a few extra ones in the closet by the kitchen, don't worry," Noah chimes in, clapping my back before I have the opportunity to respond. There's a sudden sense of relief I'm not used to, a sense of comfort and longing for that sense of family, love, and support that I didn't even realize I've missed my whole life.

***

The lights lining the roadway to the local bar are insane. I feel like I've stepped into the serene scene of a snow globe, similar to the one that was at one of the foster houses I was in. You flip it upside down, the snow flies, glitters, music plays, and the celebration begins. I wasn't allowed to take part in the celebration.

My throat tightens as I remember sitting just outside the living room, watching as the rest of the family smiled and laughed together, ate snacks, and opened presents. The kids shrieked with excitement as they opened their model cars and dolls. I felt like a fly on the wall, waiting for something to come down and squash me, for good.

The music becomes louder as we pull into the snow-covered parking lot. There is a fire pit, surrounded with people, the flame reflecting off the lake, where a group of teenagers are playing street hockey.

"I absolutely need to learn that," I say, getting out of the car.

"What? Street hockey?" Noah replies.

"Hockey, or whatever the hell they're doing," I say as one of the kids scores a goal and everyone around him dog piles him to the ice. Having that kind of bond is something I can only hope to achieve in the army. In reality, something is better than nothing, and I can tell this friendship with Noah is going to be something special.

"You're going to break your hip before getting deployed."

"I don't care." I've always lived on thrill and adrenaline, which is what got me here in the first place, getting myself in trouble before I even knew what trouble or consequences were. Hockey seems worth the risk with little long-term consequences.

Noah just laughs and shakes his head. "Come on, let's get a drink."

It's loud, I can hear the crowd from outside, laughing, singing, joking, maybe even dancing, based on the rhythmic taps I can hear on the floor. But as soon as the jingle of the doorbell goes off, everyone stops. It's gone from a loud bustling bar to a silent stare down. I assume everyone is looking at the newcomer, and I just continue to the closest open table with my best friend. I learned at a very young age that when you are a foster kid, the one with a different background, everyone is going to stare and everyone is going to talk.

"Kneland, why does that guy look like he's going to murder you?" There's this tall, lanky guy, probably our age, giving Noah a death stare over his shoulder, white-knuckling the beer bottle in his hand. There's something about this slightly off-putting guy, mean even. It's then that I notice Noah is standing next to our bar table, just frozen. He drops his head and gives the guy a curt nod.

"That's Ollie's brother," he says, almost ashamed or scared. I can't place the emotion with him yet.

This guy sets his beer bottle on the bar and pushes his stool back, getting up from the bar and walking toward us. He stalks menacingly to our table and stops directly in front of Noah. He stands at six-foot-five, so he makes Noah look small. He stands there silently for what feels like an eternity before jamming a finger into Noah's chest, uttering, "You fucked up," before bumping into him and stalking out the side door of the bar.

"Man, what the hell was that?" I demand. "I know something happened with Olivia when she didn't come back to the hotel after graduation, but what was it?"

"Nothing," he replies coldly.

"If I'm going to have to defend your ass in a bar against that man, I need to know why," I reply with a slight chuckle, trying to make a little bit of light of a serious situation. I've always been the jokester and have never responded well to conflict or sadness, but I know that whatever happened between Noah and Olivia must be serious, and he needs me more than ever.

"We need more Jameson for that story," he replies without even looking up from the table.

I push my chair back, making this god awful, ear-curling screech sending everyone in the bar looking at us yet again, but I keep my head high and my chest tall as I walk over to the bar where the beautiful bartender is standing leaning at the edge.

She has long raven colored hair that's straight as an arrow and pulled into a ponytail. She looks up from her phone at me with a devious grin. Her eyes are dark brown, warm, and comforting, like the first cup of coffee in the morning.

"Well, hello there. You must be new here. What can I get for you?"

"Me?" I ask, looking around me as if a million people were buying for her attention. "You mean you don't remember me from our amazing night together?"

She laughs with the biggest and most beautiful smile I've ever seen. After years of being disappointed and bouncing between homes and the streets, I don't get to see many genuine smiles, and this is one I vow to never forget. Her smile is like seeing the stars sparkling in the night sky for the first time. Mesmerizing. Captivating, and I am unable to look away.

"Jarred," I say, reaching my hand across the bar.

"Julie," she replies, shaking my hand hard.

Damn. Beautiful and strong.

"Well, Jarred, what brings you to Fisher Creek?"

"That sad sap over there," I say, sliding slightly to the right so she can see Noah sitting on a barstool, still looking down at the table. "Four shots of Jameson, please."

"Ah, so you know Kneland," she says, grabbing the shot glasses from underneath the bar.

"Yes? Do you?"

"Oh, honey, this is a small town, bartenders know everything. We are the gatekeepers for everyone's deepest, darkest secrets."

Not knowing how to respond, I just give her a smile.

"And I bet you have plenty." She leans over the bar, whispering into my ear, while sliding the shots along to the counter to me.

"Oh, you have no idea, but they're too dark for someone as pretty as you," I say, handing her my card. "You can close it out."

She says nothing as she runs my card and slides the receipt across the bar top for a signature. Her hand is covering the top aspect of the receipt. She pulls her hand away, smiles slyly, and heads to the other end of the bar to help another patron.

Call me if you're staying in town a bit, the note says with her phone number across the top. A smile creeps across my face, as I've never had someone leave their number for me on a receipt. Then again, I've never really had the opportunity. Usually, it's me hitting on a waitress and having them openly reject me, but this is different. There's something about Julie that grabs my attention, that keeps me engaged, but from a distance. I quickly slide the receipt into my pocket and bring the shots back to our table.

But I can't help the little pep that's now in my steps.

I was *noticed*.

I know I'm fit and considered an attractive guy, but I have never been noticed before, in a way that feels like I am wanted. It's always whispers behind my back, walking down the hallway, *"his parents didn't want him,"* and *"he must be bad news if he is out on the streets,"* or *"stay away from him."* Here, I'm someone more than the kid on the streets. I'm Jarred, the guy in the army, or Kneland's friend; and that's new but like a breath of fresh air, I didn't know I need.

I place two of the Jameson shots in front of Noah and collect myself before settling back in my chair, when I realize he hasn't moved a single muscle. He has no idea the interaction with Julie just happened behind him, and based on his current state of mind, it's probably best it stays that way.

"I broke up with Ollie," he says quietly, almost a mumble, after taking the first shot in one giant gulp.

"What? Why?"

"She came to graduation, and all she talked about was what was next for us. Where she would move, what our life together would look like, and how we are going to make it work. She had everything planned out. Except for the last five years I've *really* known her, she's wanted nothing more than to leave Fisher Creek, become a physician, and make a difference in someone's life. But she hasn't talked about her goals, schooling, or any plans for the future. She's going to give up all her dreams to be an army wife, and I cannot and will not let her do that."

I sit there staring at him, and for a moment, I half expect my jaw to be on the floor. He actually did that? Noah drags his finger along the rim of his glass, waiting for me to say something. But I have no words.

I shift elbows bracing on the table, leaning closer across the table as if I am telling him a secret.

"You know I love you, right?" I start to say, pausing as I try to find the right words. "You're an idiot. Noble as hell. But an idiot," I say after a brief pause, realizing the details were over.

He exhales, slowly, running his hands over the front of his face, silently. When he looks at me again, I finally see it, the exhaustion that has taken over, as if breaking up with Olivia has consumed his every thought and breath since graduation.

Is that why he left immediately with his family? I thought he wanted to spend as much as possible with them, maybe he just needed some personal time to work through this. Which clearly did not work.

I am in utter disbelief. I've spent the last ten weeks with him, listening to him talk about this beautiful girl he fell in love with back home, watching him write letters to her, and the smile and giddiness on his face when he got one in return.

And this man just broke up with her so she wouldn't give up her dreams. That is love. It is stupid. But it is love. I operate on: *if you love someone or something, you hold on to it tight, because you never know when it might get ripped away from you.* Especially in our field.

"I get why you did it, but damn, dude," I say, looking at him, his head tilted down, reliving that very minute where he broke the heart of the love of his life, but simultaneously his own, on all fronts.

"Are you going to tell her brothers what happened?"

"No, Carter's always hated me, and Cole is...was...my best friend, but Ollie is his sister, and can't keep a secret if his life depends on it. Telling him would lead to Olivia knowing the truth and trying to talk me out of it. It's just easier this way. Easier if they all hate me."

He picks up his final shot, throws it down his throat, tipping his head back, and slams it on the table.

"I'm sorry, I'm not really interested in drinking anymore. I think I'm just going to head home," he says, looking utterly defeated, tired, and drowning in his thoughts.

"Hold on, let me finish this and we can go."

"Stay, hang out here, experience the small town. Karaoke is about to start." This at least brings him the slightest smile, he knows I've never participated in karaoke but also love an opportunity to sing and dance.

But something is tugging at me, back over by the bar, urging me to pick a place over there.

"Are you sure? I don't mind going back to the house."

"Yeah, I need some space, and you deserve to have a true small town experience. Call me when you're ready and I'll come get you."

"Couldn't stay away, huh?" I hear her say as she walks back down the bar, dragging her fingertips along the edge of the counter toward me. I can't look away or even think of words to say in response, fulling encapsulated by the sound of her voice. A voice that is warm, bright, and impossible to ignore.

"Hard to stay away from the most beautiful girl in the place."

"Wanted to know if you want to have a drink with me when your shift is done."

"And why would I do that?"

"Well, you left me your number, and it's hard to say no to this face."

"Ha, that's fair, you do have a pretty face."

"One drink, Jules, then I'll be on my way."

"One drink with one rule," she says, leaning completely across the bar

"And that is?"

She leans so close I can feel the warmth from her breath tickling my neck, whispering in my ear. "Don't fall in love with me."

I scoff at her rule. "I don't do love."

A smirk rolls onto her face as she turns back to the bar as she says, "You haven't met me yet."

7

I said I don't love, but I think Julie is going to give me a run for my money.

She finishes her shift and saunters around the bar wearing black jeans, a black V-neck with a brown leather jacket over top, and these boots.

Boots that are the same shade as her raven hair with a little heel.

Boots that make her already-toned legs more mesmerizing, and it's all I can manage to shake the image of them wrapping around my shoulders.

Never has a pair of boots had me ready to drool over a woman before. Like a feral fucking dog.

"Whiskey on the rocks," she says, handing me a glass before taking the spot next to me at the high-top table where I'm watching these average joes attempt to sing as if they were the next stars on *American Idol*.

They completely transformed this small section at the far end of the bar into a warm, welcoming karaoke nook. The old projector screen slides down the wall, with a table for "DJ" Parker, a speaker, and two microphones. They created a comfy ambiance by hanging additional string lights along the ceiling and walls to pair with the neon karaoke sign.

You can tell these locals drop by after work or during weekend nights, not to chase fame, cause let's be honest, can you truly become famous in a small town? But they come for the joy of singing and being together. Voices echo through the speakers as the first few townies begin their renditions of "Girls Just Wanna Have Fun" and "Since You've Been Gone." Some voices are actually *Idol*-worthy, others not so much, but everyone shouts and cheers as they finish, no matter the performer.

I feel the brush of hair against the back of my forearm as Julie leans closer to me as if trying to tell me a secret.

"That couple over there," she points, keeping her hand close to her body to be discreet, " he's head-over-heels in love with her, but all she cares about is her job. She's absolutely answering emails as he tries to talk to her right now."

"What? How do you know that?"

"I don't, I just like to tell a story about the people who come to this bar for food and karaoke on a Tuesday night."

"You like to people watch?" I ask, remembering all the times I sat on the street, watching the people go by, telling a story about what they do for work, who they love, if they're loved, and if anyone ever notices a young boy with a backpack on the street day after day.

"My family owns this place and the bed and breakfast next door, so before I was able to work, this was the best way to pass the time," she says with a shrug as if it was just a natural and normal occurrence.

"Well, that guy over there, he just got back from a business trip and is sports betting while his wife dances with a stranger."

"Ah, yes, do you think the Bucks have the over tonight?" she says, mimicking the guy leaning against the wall, nose deep in his phone with one foot on the wall looking entirely uninterested in his surroundings, aside from leaning over to the guy next to him to ask a question before going clinking back on his phone again.

"The Bucks and the *over*...that's asking a lot, Rowe," I say, forgetting I'm supposed to be in character. That's just the essence of her, so beautiful, so kind, and that laugh—the laugh I only heard a snippet of earlier tonight when she was working, but I vow to have it ingrained in my brain by the end of it. She makes it so easy to forget where I am, who I am.

She pauses, looking confused. "How'd you know my last name?"

Oh, shit. I look like the creepiest guy here now.

"I, uh, well, you said your parents owned this place, and their names are on the wall with their awards. So I just kind of assumed. Sorry."

She instantly bursts into that laughter. "Relax, Jarred, I'm kidding, I know my name is plastered all over this building. But it only seems fair that I know your last name if you're going to call me mine."

"Schmidt," I say. "And that was mean, I thought you were going to ship me off to the small-town mafia." I can't get her laugh out of my head.

"I couldn't risk such a pretty face."

"So you think I'm pretty?" I say, winking at her

"I think I want to punch your *pretty* face now," she says, shaking her head with a sly smile on her face.

Her smile is bright, carefree, and all-encompassing. Like, when the sun comes out after a big storm and can't help the draw toward it. Her laugh is warm, soft, but a full-bodied laugh, the type of sound that makes you smile as soon as you hear it, full of pure joy. I will do anything and everything it hear that sound on an endless look for the remainder of the night.

"You see that guy over there?" She leans in close with a mischievous grin on her face.

I nod slightly.

"Best sex I've ever had."

I scoff, choking on my whiskey. "You haven't met me yet," I say, throwing her words back at her.

Her grin only grows, as if she has had this planned the entire time. "Guess you better show me," she replies with a gentle shrug and turns, jogging out of the bar.

Slamming the remainder of my drink and throwing a few dollars on the table, I sprint after her.

The cold air hits my face, reminding me we're in Wisconsin in December. The snow is thick and wet, slowing me down with each step as I sink through layer after layer. The wind is howling, creating an echo and wind tunnel through the trees lining the path to a warmly lit building. An old building that I hadn't noticed before. Julie is running ahead of me, giggling, as I gain ground on her.

I feel like a child again, watching kids have fun, playing tag at recess, smiling, laughing endlessly not a care in the world. Only this time, I actually get to play. And I won't let my first time be a loss.

"I'm competitive, Jules, this won't stop till I'm the best you've ever had," I call after her through the wind.

"You'll have to catch me first," she squeals before taking off even faster.

My boots are heavy, and I can see her bound up the four steps to the old historic building.

And then she's gone.

I slow as I approach the deck, scanning for any sign of where she might have gone off to, but it's too dark, making it difficult to see. The warm, orangey light is shining through the windows but they are frosted for the holidays making the window almost opaque to the light. But I would have seen more light if she opened the front door, right?

Where could she have gone?

There is a quick flash of movement on the deck before a ball of white is hurdling through the air toward my chest. Followed by more giggling from her hiding place behind the pillar. She would be terrible at hide-and-seek. Her giggling is the noise coming from behind the pillar, and it just warms my heart, making it impossible to leave this moment.

I want time to freeze right here in this moment and engrain it deep into my brain *forever*.

That damn F word. Nothing is forever in my book, and I need to remember that. No one stays forever. Forever can't happen here, she is here in Wisconsin, and before we know it, I will be overseas.

In the next second, the snowball bursts against my chest into a million different pieces, toppling into the ground. I've never seen snow before coming here, let alone a snowball or having a snowball fight, but I can absolutely understand the hype behind it. This feels exhilarating, a game of cat and mouse, hide-and-seek, with a hint of war alongside it.

But now it's time for this cat to catch his mouse.

"Ow, you wound me, Jules," I say, clutching my chest.

She stops giggling and her face molds into a serious concern mug.

"Oh my gosh, are you okay?" she says, coming closer.

"Weak, Rowe, that was too easy," I say, before scooping her over my shoulder and heading inside.

"Put me down, pretty boy, or we aren't getting into any of the rooms here." I pause for a second as a couple stands behind the desk, shaking their heads, laughing.

"Key for 204, please," Julie asks nicely, and the woman hands her a small keychain with a literal key.

"Don't hotels use key cards nowadays? Also, why didn't they take any of your information?" I ask, baffled at what I just witnessed.

Jules grabs my hand, saying nothing, leading me down the dark hallway.

"204 is my room, I basically own the room and then rent it out as necessary, but tonight, it's ours."

She unlocks the door and pushes it open, revealing a quaint, quiet room, overlooking the woods on the back side of the property. The room is dark, full of neutral colors with a pop of dark green. It doesn't feel like a standard hotel or bed and breakfast. There is a homey feeling to it; warm and welcoming.

She shrugs off her leather jacket, tossing it to the large green chair in the corner of the room, which sits next to a golden overhead lamp. She turns back around, revealing the square-neck tank top that cups her chest perfectly.

With a sly upturn of one corner of her mouth, she sits in the chair, bending at her waist just enough to take her heeled boots on, and knows exactly what she is doing.

My arousal is already building just by looking at how beautiful she is, and she says, "Pretty sure you were going to prove to me how you're the best lay I'll ever have."

"Honey, you have no idea what you're getting yourself into." I cross the short distance from the entryway to the chair and drop to my knees before her.

Reaching my hands to her leg, I unzip her heeled boot, she sucks in a gasp of air, and I know that I am already moving in the right direction.

"These things will be the death of me one day," I whisper, placing a kiss on the inside of her knee.

"My boots?" she gasps again.

"These boots, these legs, that ass," I say between kisses up her leg as I slide the first heel off and begin working on the second.

Kneeling between her legs, I cup either side of her ass and slide her to the edge of the chair, wanting, needing her closer to me.

She places one hand around the back of my neck pulling me closer, the other hand clamped onto my forearm.

"Jarred," she whispers.

"Yes?" I say, placing a kiss on her collarbone as she arches into me.

"Take my clothes off," she barely gets out before I find the button to her jeans and reveal her black lace underwear that matches her silky hair.

"Fuck, you're beautiful," I croak, memorizing her body, the shape of her curves, the feel of her skin.

"If you don't touch me in the next three seconds, I'm going to do it myself and make you watch," she demands, already writhing in anticipation and need.

"Don't worry, Rowe, I'm going to find all the places you like to be touched, but I'm going to take my time doing it," I say, placing a kiss on the inside of her knee.

"No," she gasps, closing her eyes.

"No? How about here? Or here?" I ask, placing kisses up the inside of her thighs, as I approach her apex.

Placing my thumb against her clit through her panties, I can feel how wet she is.

"You're so wet, Jules. I can't wait to know what you taste like," I say as I slide her panties to the side before dipping my tongue inside.

She whimpers at the contact, and my dick instantly twitches. I keep working my tongue inside her, reaching another hand beneath her shirt to roll her nipple between my fingers.

"Shit, Jarred, I'm close," she gasps, arching into my face.

"Good, be a good girl and come on my face," I say, before diving a finger inside her and licking perfect circles around her clit.

We ride her orgasm out together, and I come up for air, pulling her orgasm-ridden body close to me to carry her to the bed.

"I want to touch you," she says reaching between her legs for my belt.

"Not yet. I'm not done with you."

Sitting on the edge of the bed, she moves her body against the length of my erection, eliciting another twitch.

Fuck, if we keep going like this I'm not going to last long. I roll us onto her back, my shaft still pressed against her middle.

She gasps, and I feel my dick grow against my jeans. It's getting to the point of uncomfortable.

"You can look but you can't touch," I say, unbuttoning my jeans.

"You're going to kill me," she says.

"No, just going to be the best you've ever had," I say, kissing my way from her beautiful pussy up to her collarbone, before gently sliding a finger into her crease. She is still so damn wet.

"Wait, should we use a condom?" She stops me.

"I got tested before basic, I'm clean, haven't been with anyone else. You?" I say, pulling back slightly.

"Same, well, not for basic, but tested last month," she says.

"Birth control?" I ask quickly.

"IUD," she replies.

"Great."

"I need you inside me, Jarred, right fucking now," she demands.

"You don't have to tell me twice, Jules, you're already so wet for me," I say before sliding into her and riding out the most magical orgasm of my life.

"What's my score?" I say, flopping onto my back, next to her, catching my breath after riding her through two perfect orgasms before finishing myself.

"Hmm, probably a seven," she says, touching her finger to her face like she's thinking.

"A *seven?* You came twice!"

"Correct, but you could probably do better."

"Oh yeah? What do you want me to do, Jules?"

"Well, you could tie my hands over my head to start," she says, kissing the side of my neck, working her way up toward my ear. "Then maybe place a hand around my neck for a little breath play," she adds as she slides open a second drawer on her nightstand, revealing a vibrator and a red cloth tie.

"Christ," I murmur, my dick instantly hard at the thought.

"You'll just have to settle for a passing score." She smirks.

"I think not. We are not stopping till I get a perfect score." Grabbing the tie from her drawer and gently tying her to the headboard, I slip down between her legs to taste the mess we made.

I will settle for nothing less than perfect, and perfect she is.

***

The warmth of her hand against my chest as we lie tangled in sheets feels like a blanket securing me into place on a rainy day. Her dark hair splayed across the pillow next to me, our breathing starting to come together as one, and I feel a sense of peace.

A part of me wants to remain here under the warmth of her touch forever.

"J," she says hesitantly.

"Jules?"

"You're amazing."

"Me? No, I'm not."

"Why do you think that?"

I'm quiet for a moment, but there's an urge inside me to tell her the truth. Give her the truth behind my story and how I ended up here in Fisher Creek.

"My life has been...hectic, for lack of a better way to explain it. My parents abandoned me on the streets of Louisiana on my seventh birthday, and none of the foster homes worked out. Some were better than others, but I got in trouble a lot. And would definitely still be on the streets if not dead if it weren't for Commander Gibson finding me right before graduation. He convinced me that there was something for me out in the world; it just took me a few years to get there."

"I'm sorry, Jarred. That's terrible. They just left you? Where are they now?"

I pause for a brief moment, deciding how to tell her.

"Oh my god, I'm sorry that was rude of me. Don't feel obligated to answer that."

Gently running my hand over her soft hair and down the bare skin of her back, I begin the story.

"Don't be sorry. I don't talk about it much, but I want to tell you. I don't remember a lot from that time. A therapist I saw at one point said my brain was blocking it out to protect myself from reliving the trauma, and that eventually I would have to work through it, thus remembering it all. In which I instantly fired them," I say with a chuckle, remembering back to that day where the super-kind, red-haired woman who just wanted to help me, stood stone still and silent when I told her to fuck off and that I would be finding someone else.

"Looking back on that now, probably not my best move. I knew she was right. I just wasn't ready to accept it yet."

She moves off my chest, propping herself up on one elbow, looking up directly at me. Her big eyes drooping with a slight glossy look to fight back tears but also listening intently.

"Basically, from what I remember, my parents struggled with addiction. We had a small one-bedroom apartment, and there would be days when I never saw them. Ruth was often completely passed out on the floor, and I was unable to wake her. James was in and out but acted as if I didn't exist. That went on for as long as I can remember until my seventh birthday. They promised me a cupcake from this little bakery down the road, and well, we got there, sat at this little booth while they went to get the cupcake...and they never came back."

"Wait, they just left you sitting at a booth in a bakery?" she asks, jaw dropped and brow furrowed with anger.

"Yeah, I don't know how long I sat there before someone finally came over to me and asked where my parents were. I said they were getting me a cupcake, but turns out I was the only one in the bakery. Police came and the rest is history."

"Did they look for or find your parents?"

"Not that I know of. The running theory is that they went to the bathroom to get high and then left out the back looking for more drugs, forgetting they left a child in a booth."

"I will never understand how someone can just forget a child. In a car, at the grocery store, at school. Running late is one thing, but to completely forget they exist? How?"

"It happens. Parenthood is definitely hard, it changes the dynamic of a household. And also was basically non-existent as it was. Add drug addiction on top of it...it's really not that farfetched. Not saying that makes it okay. But I see it happening. Hell, I lived it."

Now it's her turn to be silent; a tear falls down her cheek, and she quickly wipes it away.

"Don't feel sorry for me, Jules. I'm okay. I don't need your pity. I got out and am going to do big things."

Another tear.

"You're so optimistic, so sure of yourself and your future with the army. You do everything to ensure the people around you maintain their peace even though you haven't known peace a day in your life."

"It's part of life. Sometimes you get dealt a bad card, and just have to ride through the game until the next card comes. It comes down to how you react to each card, control what you can, let go of what you can't."

I wrap my other arm around her hip rolling her closer into my, feeling her warmth along my bare chest, and hold her tight.

"I can control this, right here, right now, my one night with you. I can choose to be here in this moment, with the most beautiful women I have ever met, instead of living inside my brain where the noise is loud and it can be dark. But...Julie, you bring the light and the quiet into that dark place. And for now, that is where I want to be."

"Jarred, you know this is can only be a one-time thing, right? You can't stay here forever," she says. "You have your entire career ahead of you, I have school and work, I'm opening a new coffee shop in town, a perfect place for tourists, but also welcoming the locals. A place that screams community. And there is no way I can do distance, not know-ing when, or even *if*, I would ever see you again. That's impossible. I don't understand how military spouses survive the constant ache."

"Forever doesn't exist in my world, Jules. I know this is a one-time thing. Doesn't mean I can't live in the moment," I pause, because after tonight, something tells me that maybe forever isn't always a bad thing. "But I do need to get back to the Knelands' house before everyone wakes up," I say, glancing at the clock. It's almost 6 a.m. at this point.

"I can drive you. Hold on, let me just get dressed," she says, starting to shimmy out of my grip.

"I don't want this night to end," I whisper into the top of her head before letting her go.

"Me either, but all great things come to an end eventually," she says as she slides on a pair of sweatpants, a black sweatshirt, and a beanie onto her head.

"Hey, Jules?" I ask, watching her finish getting ready as I start to tie my boots back up.

"Yeah?"

"Let's keep this our little secret. I don't want it to affect your life, living in a small town."

"Oh hell, Jarred, they can't create gossip when I control the gossip. You don't have to worry. Our secret is safe."

There's a little bite to her words that stings like a slap to the face. But I know she's right, she can definitely take care of herself. She is strong, independent, fun, and so fucking beautiful.

How am I going to just walk away from her?

"Ready?" she asks, standing at the door of her room.

"Almost," I say, stepping closer, pushing one arm against the door over her head, keeping it closed, while pushing her back against the door, using my index finger to lift her chin and brush my thumb along her bottom lip.

"One last kiss, to seal the best night," I say before kissing her slowly and deeply.

Intimate. More intimate than any kiss I have ever wanted before.

She sucks in a breath before arching into me, returning the kiss.

I pull away, wiping my mouth, and lower my hand into my pocket.

"Okay, ready," I say, and we walk out the door.

More snow has fallen overnight, and we pass people shoveling the pathways and park before it gets busy for the day. They all smile and wave at Julie, addressing her as Miss Rowe.

She returns the gesture, asking them about their day, knowing them all by name, and I can't help but think about how amazing she is. To everyone around her, to herself, to me, the grounds crew.

We ride in silence, dreading the final goodbye of our night together. On multiple occasions, I resist the urge to slide my hand over to her thigh. Wanting to be closer to her more and more, the closer we get to goodbye.

She turns down the long dirt driveway leading to the Knelands' house, and I hear a sad sigh followed by a gulp of emotions. This is hard for her, too. If I believed in love at first sight this might be what it feels like. What I imagine it looks like, too. But love at first sight is only something that happens in movies, and this isn't a movie.

"I fear you might be my favorite person, J," I say, getting out of her car in Noah's driveway.

I swear I hear her mumble, "You might be mine, too," before I shut the door and prepare to never see her again.

I feel an ache in my chest that tightens at the thought. This is the right thing to do, but even sitting in silence, both sad the entire drive back to Noah's, there was a pull toward her. My entire body stuck to a magnet attracted only to her.

Everyone is still asleep when I get in the house, surprised by the door being unlocked. That feels exceptionally unsafe, and I make a mental note to remind Noah of that when the sun comes up. When I take off my borrowed jacket, I notice there's a piece of paper in the pocket I don't remember being there. Sliding it out, I realize there's something written on it.

J, if you ever need a person to take some of the noise, I'm your girl. We'll call it pen pals.

Creek and Kettle, Attn: J Rowe, 143 Main Street, Fisher Creek, Wisconsin

"What are you smiling at? Also, are you just getting home?" Noah says, yawning as he walks into the living room.

"Yeah, I met some locals, and watched karaoke. Stayed at the B and B. Just looking at the receipt." A half-truth, kind of. I've never been a great liar, which is mostly why I was constantly in trouble as a kid.

"Aww, look at you making friends, I told you you'd never forget Fisher Creek," he says with a chuckle.

You have no idea.

8

"I need caffeine. I hear there's a new coffee shop opening downtown today. Want to check it out?" Noah asks, running his hand through his messy hair as he yawns.

"Sure," I reply. "I could probably use a pick-me-up."

"What's the new shop called, Mom?" he calls into the kitchen as if we aren't standing in the next room over of an open concept house.

Martha is sitting at the breakfast table with her feet up, glasses sliding down the bridge of her nose, reading the newspaper. Without missing a beat, she calls back, "Creek and Kettle. Mark and Melinda's youngest is opening it. I swear that girl is just like her mama. Driven and ambitious as hell."

My cheeks heat, and I turn toward the cabinet, pretending I need a glass of water to hide the redness.

That's Julie's shop. When she it was opening soon, I didn't think she meant today. That girl stayed out all night with me when her new shop, her dream business, is having its grand opening today.

She's incredible.

But she made it clear that last night was a one-time thing. Would she be upset if I came to the grand opening? I mean, she didn't even tell me that it was happening, so how was I supposed to know? Yep, exactly that, I'm just going to play dumb.

Except, I can't help but imagine her behind the counter wearing a pair of black leggings, a slouchy long-sleeve shirt, with her hair tied in a messy bun atop her head. Wearing a lilac color apron on and that darn smile that lights up the entire room.

"Hello, earth to Jarred, you there?" Noah asks, pulling me out of my daydream.

"Oh, yeah. Sorry, what?"

"I asked if that worked? Do you want to go? I went to high school with the Rowe's and it'd be nice to support baby Rowe."

Baby Rowe? What kind of nickname was that? How many Rowe's were there? I guess we didn't talk much about her outside of her coffee shop. But c'mon, she's a beautiful, whole ass adult, let's not call her baby Rowe. At least not while I'm remembering my head between her thighs. *Gross.*

"Oh yeah, that's fine with me. Just need to shower."

"Sweet, it looks like it opened at seven," Noah says, looking at his phone and pulling up the social media account for Creek and Kettle.

I learned that parking in a small town is almost just as bad as parking in a city, there are few to no spots, and most of it is street parking. The street is lined with cars, parked in angled spots, and then there is a small lot at the end of the street, where you can park before walking to the stores downtown.

We're fortunate enough to get a spot in that lot, sliding into it as someone's leaving with a tray of coffee and a baggie, presumably containing pastries. *God, I hope it's pastries.* My stomach grumbles lightly in response.

This town reminds me of one of those Hallmark movies all the girls watch around the holidays, especially with the light dusting of new snow. The only thing missing is Christmas decorations, but I am sure those will be out before you know it. The sidewalk is damp and sprinkled with various salt pellets that crunch under our boots. There is a mixture of older brick buildings and buildings that consist of your stereotypical siding.

There is a line of people outside the door in the middle of the line of buildings, where the doorframe is lined with two beautiful balloon pillars. The balloons are a mixture of sage green, white, and a light gray to accept the over-the-door grand opening banner with the *Creek & Kettle* logo. I smile at the line of people, a sense of pride coming over me seeing all of these people waiting for a coffee here to support Jules.

"Jesus, it's packed," I say as we approach the line outside the giant front window to the store.

"That's the power of a small town, everyone knows everyone. And everyone knows the Rowes especially," Noah replies. My face must scream confusion because he goes on. "Mark and Melinda Rowe own Fishy's Bar and the Bed and Breakfast next to it. They're also the biggest sponsors for the school system, providing supplies and sports equipment each year. Everyone in town has benefited from the Rowes' kindness over the years and are always wanting to pay it back."

"That's really cool." I've never been in a community where people are constantly working to help the people around them. The best I've seen was Antonio offering me a job. My high school didn't have a small business that sponsored or donated to it, and if it did, I didn't know about it.

Looking in the window, the shop's completely full, and there's Julie, standing behind the counter with a lilac apron, a giant smile as she chats mindlessly with the patron in front of her. There's a tall woman who could be her twin standing behind the counter, and two men with lighter hair, standing with their backs to us, working at the back counter to box up treats.

"There is small army of them working in there," I say, not realizing I say it out loud, mesmerized by the efficiency with which they work together, all smiling and laughing.

"That's the Rowe crew for you. Julianna, the owner, is the one making drinks – you might recognize her from the bar last night. She makes the best drinks in town. Her sister is behind the register, and then her dad and brother are the other two behind the counter. Julie is the youngest, Justin was in school with me, and Jess is older than all of us. And if I had to guess, Melinda is probably inside the door, greeting everyone. They all stayed in town to help run the family businesses and support the community. Jess and Justin both went to college online, and I imagine that's probably the route Julianna is taking," Noah replies.

Julianna? Is that her full name? I wonder why she introduced herself as Julie to me.

"I'm having a hard time believing there are families like that."

"Surprisingly, that's the norm for Fisher Creek."

My gaze keeps drifting back to the girl with raven hair as she bends across the counter, getting another shot of espresso. The wide smile never once leaves her face, even as the crowd grows, and things spill. She takes it all in stride and doesn't falter once.

I'm here for the coffee, so Kneland can support the grand opening, and whatever pastry smells delicious. But I can't ignore my heart beating faster every time she smiles, a smile that seems too easy, with those warm coffee-colored eyes.

We round the corner through the front door and are met by a woman, who looks like a slightly older version of Julie and her sister. It's almost freaky how similar they all are, the genes certainly run strong in that family.

"Hi, Melinda!" Noah says, sticking out his arm for a handshake.

"Noah Kneland! You know we hug here. I can't believe you're home," she says pulling him into a quick familiar hug. "And who is this?" she asks, raising an eyebrow at me.

"Jarred Schmidt, ma'am," I say, holding out my hand to her.

"Oh god, please, don't call me ma'am. Melinda is perfect," she says, taking my hand. "How long are you visiting, Jarred?"

"Just for a few days, we have to report in Arizona at the end of the week," I reply.

Thankfully, a table in the corner against a giant exposed brick wall, and the front window opens, so we leave Melinda and head over to sit down.

"Do you know what you want?" I ask Noah, as he quietly mingles with the people at the table next to us.

"Oh, you should definitely get the pumpkin spice latte," the lady says, looking at Noah. "Julianna designs the cutest pumpkin with the foam on the top."

Julianna—there it is again.

"I could go for that, it is fall, right?" he says.

"Cool, I'll grab them and be back."

For the grand opening, Julie's created a specialty menu, and for every drink you purchase, you receive a small box of assorted pastries, or at least that's what the sign says. As I stand in line, my stomach starts to turn, wondering if this is a good idea. Maybe I should've let Noah get the drinks.

"Hi, what can I get for you?" Julie's sister asks.

"Hi, uh, can I get the pumpkin patch latte and the harvest spice cold brew?"

"What size, hon?" she asks kindly.

"Oh, um... medium is good," I reply, sneaking a glance to the left where Julie is bent down making a design on the latte in front of her.

"Perfect, that'll be $10. You're not from around here, are you?" she asks with a sly smile on her face.

"No, ma'am, visiting the Kneland family," I reply, handing her some cash. "You can keep the change."

"Thank you," she says, softening her smile as she waves me to follow the counter to the left.

"Pretty boy, what are you doing in my coffee shop on this delightful morning?" Julie asks without even looking up from her work.

"How'd you know it was me?"

"I remember everything, especially the voice of..." She pauses, looking around us, then leans in and quietly finishes, "a=A man whose face was between my legs not even eight hours ago."

I chuckle, giving her a soft smile.

"Kneland wanted caffeine and to support the infamous Rowes. I promise I'm not stalking you. Although I am a little hurt you didn't tell me the opening was today."

Julie's hands move like a dance to hiss of milk, the golden stream of espresso. Each movement measured, fluid, and certain. Watching her hands feels intimate, like I'm witnessing a magical act in a language I don't speak.

"Are you watching my hands, Schmidt?" she asks, smirking at me.

My face clearly reddens, and I see her sister smile out of the corner of my eyes.

"You're talented, J," I say in response.

By the time the cup slides across the counter, I'm wondering if it's the caffeine I'm craving, or simply Julie.

9

We're enjoying our coffees, Noah talking to the people around him. I'm trying to be discreet watching Julie as she creates masterpiece after masterpiece. It's truly like the whole town came out to support her.

Noah's phone rings, and I see a glimpse of a photo of a young girl across his screen—Bec.

"Hey, Bec, what's up?" he answers.

I turn back to my coffee and the counter, where I make subtle eye contact with Julie for the first time since ordering. Her smile spans the entire width of her face before she jumps back into her routine.

"Yeah, let me see what Schmidt wants to do and I'll let you know," Noah says before hanging up and turning to me.

I raise an eyebrow at him at the mention of my name.

"Since we won't be home for Christmas, Bec wants to do our annual ski day trip this weekend while I'm home. Want to go?"

I pause. I have no idea how to ski. Hell, this is my first real experience with snow. It would be a cool opportunity to try something new. But there's also this ache inside me, telling me to stay. To see if Julie is free and would want to hang out.

"I don't know how to ski," I say.

"We can teach you," he replies with a promising look on his face.

"No, no, you go and spend time with Bec. I don't want to impose, plus, I'm sure I can find something around here to do," I reply.

Noah narrows his eyes at me, before saying, "Are you sure? We'll only be gone for the day tomorrow, then have all of Sunday before heading out on Monday."

"Yes, Kneland. I'm sure," I say, crossing my arms over my chest, fighting the smirk itching to come across my face as I glance back at Julie.

"What are you going to do?" he asks, skepticism and concern reaching his eyes.

"Kneland, I have spent the majority of my life alone. I'm sure there are plenty of things to do in this small town. I'll find something. Go have fun." I say in a firm tone, almost as if scolding him. But in reality, it's the only way to actually get him to go. I'll find something to do.

I have just the thing in mind.

"I'm going to run to the bathroom and then say hi to Mark before we leave," Noah says, getting up from the table.

I nod in response, taking the last sip from my coffee as he walks down the narrow hallway toward the restroom.

"Are you all set with these?" a soft, familiar voice says.

I look up to see Julie standing next to the table, ready to bus our dishes.

"Yes, ma'am," I reply, unable to hide my smile. As her arm reaches out to pick up each glass, I realize this is my chance—and probably the only chance I'm going to have. "Jules?" I ask.

"J?" she responds, pausing as she looks down at me.

"Are you doing anything tomorrow? Kneland's going skiing with Bec."

Her smile grows and her coffee brown eyes twinkle. "Just can't get enough, can you?" she says.

"Hey, I told you I've never been good at following the rules."

She shakes her head, continuing to smile.

"What do you say, Jules? Show me what it's like to live in a small town in Wisconsin," I say, placing my hand over hers on the table.

"Two p.m. Here. Don't be late," she replies, sliding her hand and glassware across the table, walking away.

I can't help but watch as she goes, hardly unable to wait an entire day before seeing her again.

***

The jingle of the door and the quiet music playing over the speaker, is an entirely different atmosphere today than yesterday at Creek and Kettle. The chaos of the grand opening is clearly quieting down as there's no one left in the shop, except for Jules, who's sitting at the counter, facing the exit, a pencil in one hand that she is gliding across the table.

"1:57 p.m, punctual, I like that," she says without looking up at the paper in front of her. As I approach, I see she's drawing, sketching rather.

"If you're not five minutes early, then you're late," I reply.

Her hair hangs in a loose braid over one shoulder, with a heather gray college sweatshirt and leggings. Her legs are crossed, and she's leaning toward the hand she's drawing with. She's carefully sketching the front of the shop with meticulous lines, depicting what it looked like yesterday, full of people.

"I said it once, and I'll say it again. You're incredibly talented, Jules."

She blushes before saying, "Thank you. I just want to remember this exactly how it was."

"It's beautiful. You did a great job. And I can say that I got to see all angles," I reply.

Her face reddens more, but she doesn't say anything.

"So, Jules, what's in store for today? What's it like living in a small town?" I ask, anxious to see what she has planned.

She looks up from me before the corner of her lips lifts into a smirk.

"You'll just have to wait and see," she replies. "But first you're going to need these," she finishes before turning to a large bag on her side and pulling out a beanie and gloves.

"A hat and gloves?" I ask.

"Yep. Come on," she says, sliding off the stool before grabbing her winter coat, personal hat, and gloves.

We drive to the outskirts of town, by what appears to be snow-covered farmlands. There's another fresh layer of snow on the ground, making it shine bright against the almost white, thick clouds coating the sky.

Julie's old car rattles as we drive, letting us feel every bump and divot in the salt-covered road. Where the sun should be shining bright above us as we chug down the narrow, winding road, we're met with overwhelmingly gloomy gray clouds.

The trees are clutching to a few rust-covered leaves, but are mostly lined with a thin layer of white snow from yesterday's snowfall. The road widens as a gravel lot appears along the right side of the road. We slow into a spot at the far side of the lot.

"What are we doing here?" I ask skeptically.

There are small groups of people bundled up, scattered across the field and hill.

"Sledding." She smiles back at me.

"Sledding?"

"Yes, pretty boy, sledding. Or are you too pretty to go sledding?"

"Ha, I don't even know what sledding is.

"What do you mean?" she says, taking my hand.

"I'm from Louisiana; we don't have snow or cold weather."

"Well, get ready to have the adventure of a lifetime," she finishes.

I turn and watch the groups of parents standing in small groups at the bottom of the hill, hands holding steaming cups, talking, laughing and smiling as they watch their children race up the steep hill, and down on little mats.

That hill is giant; what constitutes the difference between a hill and a mountain? I'm not sure what makes me more nervous, the fact that the hill looks more like a crazy ski jump or that Julie's smile made it nearly impossible to back out of this.

"Come on," she calls over her shoulder, tugging the blue plastic sled like it weighs nothing. Where did she even get that? I was too concerned watching the kids go down the hill to even see her pull it out. Her boots crunch through the top layer of snow where the sun melted and refroze. "It's not scary. It's fun."

"Fun," I mutter, slipping for the third time as I follow her up the slope. "Where I come from, 'fun' is sneaking into a movie theater to escape the heat and humidity, not hurling yourself down an icy hillside."

She laughs, the sound carrying over the hill, and I swear it warms me more than my coat.

At the top, she drops the sled onto the snow and turns, cheeks pink, warm brown eyes dancing with that daredevil glint. "Okay, pretty boy. Front or back?"

"Is neither an option?"

"How else do you plan to get down this hill? I sure as hell am not trekking down it."

I sigh, a deep sigh that comes all the way from my toes, knowing that she's won. But she will always win with me.

"Fine. Back." I lower myself onto the sled, stiff as a board, while she sits in front of me. The lilac and coconut smell of her hair wafting into my nose, causing me to want to wrap my arms around her waist and nestle my nose in the crook of her neck. Every nerve in my body lights up, and suddenly, the snow doesn't feel cold at all.

"Ready?" she asks, almost yelling so I hear her over the steady wind in the air.

"Absolutely not."

"Perfect." She puts her hand into the snow and throws us forward before I even have a second to blink.

The world blurs around me, snow flying into my face, my stomach drops, the sled careening faster than I thought humanly possible. A yell escapes me, and definitely not in a cool way, more of a "holy fuck am I going to live way" but also in a "this is an adrenaline rush and I need more" way. Jules laughs, the same free, bubbling sound that cut straight through my chest last night.

And then, somehow, I'm laughing, too. Scared out of my mind, half convinced we're about to die—but laughing.

I close my eyes as we skid to a stop at the bottom, spraying snow everywhere. My heart hammers, and I open my eyes to find her looking at me, grinning so wide my chest aches.

"See?" she says, breathless. "Pure joy."

I shake my head, unable to find the words. "You're insane. Completely insane. But...yeah. That was..." I pause, searching for the right words to describe how I feel, and ultimately decide to land on the truth. "Incredible."

She leans in, brushing a clump of snow from my hair, her glove trailing against my temple just a beat longer than necessary. "Told you." Her smile softens, and for a second, I forget the sled, the hill, even the snow.

"Now," she yells, jumping up, "round two."

I groan, but she already has my hand and is leading us back up the hill. "You're going to kill me before I even get to training."

She squeezes my fingers, her smile turning almost shy. "Or I'm going to make sure you never forget today."

And just like that, I know she's right.

***

From the top of the hill, you can see the dirt parking lot, the narrow two-lane road, and then what overlooks the town and the lake in the far distance. As the sun starts to set behind the clouds, you can see hues of purple starting to bleed through the gray as the area around us begins darkening.

We finish another ride down the hill, laughing just as hard as the first time, when I feel Jules's body tremble against me.

"Are you cold?" I ask, realizing the temperature's dropping quickly.

"Maybe a little," she hesitates in response as her teeth impulsively chatter, giving her away.

"Come on, let's go back to town and grab something to eat and warm up." I place my hand along the small of her back, grabbing the sled string from her hand as we head back toward to rickety old car.

"I have an idea," I say, putting her in the passenger seat, before getting in the driver's seat to drive.

"You don't have to drive, Jarred. It's my car, I'll drive."

"I have no doubt in my mind that you can drive, but you're freezing and can barely keep your body still. Let me do this, I want to drive us back."

She rolls her eyes at me before silently agreeing and settling into her seat.

"Have you ever made homemade tomato soup?" I ask, reaching over the center console and placing my hand on her thigh.

"I don't think I've ever made soup, period. Why would I make it when I can just buy a can at the grocery store?"

I smile. "It's a thousand times better homemade. Can you direct me to the closest grocery store?"

She looks at me with a blank stare, as if I've completely lost my mind.

"You're not the only one making this day unforgettable."

Jules rolls her eyes at me again, trying to hide the shy smile on her face, but completely gives it away when she gently squeezes my hand where it sits on her thigh.

Her cheeks are still pink from the cold when we step into the kitchen, our boots dripping snow by the door, but at least the chattering of her teeth and trembling of her body have stopped. She's grinning, hair tangled and wet from the wind and the snow.

I can't help but smile back, even though my shoulders ache from colliding with the hill one too many times.

"All right," I say, discarding my sweatshirt and jacket on the hood by the door. "You're about to learn the secret to surviving winter."

"You're from Louisiana, you don't even have a winter," she counters.

"It still gets chilly in Louisiana, Jules."

She leans against the counter, skeptical but curious. "Tomato soup and grilled cheese? That's your big secret?"

I gasp, offended. "It's not *just* tomato soup. It's homemade tomato soup. And the best grilled cheese you'll ever have." I toss her the apron hanging on the pantry. "Suit up, Jules."

She laughs as she fumbles with the ties, and I pull the cans of tomatoes from the shopping bag.

The pan hisses when I drop in butter and garlic, the smell filling the room. She watches me stir, standing behind me, peering around the side of my arm. I can feel her warmth against the bare skin of my arm, but also through the T-shirt I'm wearing.

"Your turn," I say, handing her the wooden spoon. "Don't let it stick."

She takes it, hesitant at first, then more confident, and I step behind her to guide her hand. My chest brushes her shoulder, and for a second I forget about the soup entirely.

"Now comes the important part," I murmur, forcing myself to step back before I burn something. I grab bread and cheese. "Grilled cheese has rules. Good bread, mayonnaise instead of butter, and never, ever, skimp on the cheese."

"Excuse me, did you just say mayonnaise?" She stops stirring and turns around with a disgusted look on her face.

"Yes, Jules, I did. Also, keep stirring," I say, stepping closer, guiding her arm in a circular motion again.

"Why on earth would you put mayonnaise on the outside of a sandwich?"

"It crisps up nicer, and the fatty components make it taste better."

She continues to look at me skeptically but returns to stirring the tomato soup. I gently stack the slices in the pan using a spatula to press them into the pan. The sizzling makes her gasp, a mixture of startle and excitement. By the time the soup's blended smooth and steaming, and the sandwiches are golden and dripping with cheese, we're both starving. We sit at the counter, and when she takes her first bite, her eyes widen.

"Okay," she says, voice muffled around the sandwich. "You weren't lying. This is…incredibly good."

I lift my spoon of soup, clink it against her bowl like a toast, and can't stop the laugh that slips out. "Told you. Trust me, you'll never go back to canned soup again."

"Where did you learn to make this?"

"Before joining the army, a man named Antonio found me squatting outside his dive bar and offered me a job, shelter, and a warm meal."

"Tomato soup?" she asks, voice quiet.

"Well, sort of. His lead bouncer, Elliot, brought me back to his house that night so I could clean up and get ready for my first shift. His wife was making homemade tomato soup and offered to teach me. It was the only thing I knew how to cook for a long time."

"That's a really sweet story, Jarred, I'm glad you found someone to help you."

"Don't thank me yet, the night is still young. Tomato soup and grilled cheese aren't the only things I learned."

Her smile reaches her eyes as she looks down at her bowl for another spoonful. I know I'm staring but really, I'm not watching her eat. I'm watching the way the steam curls between us, the way the flush from the cold still lingers on her skin, and thinking that maybe the real secret to survival is her sitting here with me.

I am brought back to reality by my phone ringing from my jacket pocket across the room. Who could possibly be calling me?

"Sorry," I stammer, standing to at least turn the ringer off. "I don't use it often and forget the ringer is on. Let me shut it off."

"It's okay, pretty boy, answer the phone. It might be important and I'll start cleaning this up."

I turn the phone over in my hand and see Noah's name across the top. *Noah.* I completely forgotten I'm staying with my best friend and that he's coming back to Fisher Creek after skiing all day. Are they back already?

"Hello?" I answer the phone.

"Hey, Schmidty, I'm so sorry, we aren't going to make it back until the morning. The mountain got a lot of snow today, and the road is closed until they can clear it in the morning. I'm sorry, dude." Noah's voice echoes over the phone, almost frantic. I can hear the sorrow in his voice.

"It's okay, man. Shit happens. We'll explore tomorrow. Just get home safe."

"Are you sure?" Noah asks skeptically.

"Yeah, it's fine. I'm just hanging out, and I'll be here when you get home in the morning."

"Okay. Thanks, Schmidt. This trip meant a lot to Bec. I've gotta go, she wants to get dinner. See you tomorrow." I can hear Bec calling for him in the background to hurry up before he hangs up the phone.

There is a sense of relief that overcomes my entire body. I can spend more time with Julie. Although I'm shocked, he didn't ask more questions about my day.

"Everything okay?" Julie asks, a genuinely concerned tone in her voice that I am not used to hearing from anyone.

"Yeah, Noah and Bec are snowed in, so they won't be back until tomorrow. So, really, it just means I don't have to rush the best part of my surprise," I say, stepping closer to her in the kitchen, wrapping my arms around her waist, nestling my chin into the crook of her neck as she stands at the sink.

"Here, why don't you go shower and get comfy with a show for us to watch, and I'll finish this and meet you with dessert."

"Dessert?" She steps to the side, eyes widening.

"You said you have a sweet tooth, and my winter survival guide isn't nearly complete yet," I say, taking the dish from her and nodding my head down the hallway of her apartment.

Her smile is wide, but also radiant, like a burst of warmth that feels like stepping into the first sunny spring day. The kind of smile that makes everything seem lighter. A smile of pure joy that threatens to disarm you before you even know what is happening.

The smile that will be burned into my memory for as long as I live.

***

Julie is lying on her stomach, setting up her laptop at the end of her bed to watch a show, still smiling as I walk into the threshold carrying two warm mugs.

"What are we watching?" I ask, hoping not to scare her.

"Well, you said you've never watched reality TV. So we have to watch a staple, *Survivor*," she exclaims, her excitement almost palpable.

"*Survivor*?" I ask.

"It's the best. A group of contestants goes to a tropical island and is split into tribes, competing in epic challenges for immunity and rewards. The winner is voted on by the contestants, who are voted out each episode in the season and wins a million dollars!"

I hand her a mug, sliding onto the side of the bed next to her, looking at her laptop, where there's this beautiful tropical scene straight out of a dream. The turquoise waters shimmer beneath the hot, bright sun, brushing up against the white sand beach that curves around the shoreline.

The scene instantly turns to this lush green forest with a rickety shack made out of...bamboo? I think it's bamboo. The person on the screen begins talking about not having food for the last five days, and I'm beginning to wonder what kind of show Julie is into.

"You mean to tell me people go out into the jungle on a tropical island to starve for the *potential* of winning a million dollars?"

"Well, yeah, it's called *Survivor* for a reason."

"It's like a one in thirty chance of getting the money, and you have to suffer for it. Doesn't seem worth it to me."

"I promise you'll love it...it's more than just suffering. It's competitive, alliances, friendships, backstabbing, drama. This show is everything," she says in response, with an innocent smile, looking up at me as she nestles closer into me, taking a small sip of her drink.

Her eyes widen as she almost gasps with disbelief.

"Jarred, what is this?"

"My secret piece of heaven."

She rolls her eyes, looking mildly annoyed. "I need you to tell me 'cause I'll need this every day for the remainder of my life. It might even be better than sex."

"Better than sex?" I say, faking offense.

"Right now it scores higher than you," she says with a little tilt of her mouth, knowing exactly how to push my buttons.

"Wow. Rude. If we didn't have hot drinks in our hands, I'd make you reconsider that number. But it's homemade hot chocolate with mini marshmallows in it."

"Not only do you make homemade soup, but homemade hot chocolate, too? Are you sure you didn't grow up in the snow?"

"Extremely. But many of my foster families had multiple kids, and we always had the packaged powder shit. That same year, I learned to make soup, Elliot's wife taught me this, too. They use the warm milk to calm their kids at night, but also a sweet little treat. It has become a comfort drink for me," I reply, looking down at her burgundy comforter, feeling vulnerable and wondering if I've shared too much information this time around.

"Well, thank you, Jarred."

"For what?"

"For sharing a piece of you so personal and real. It can't be easy but giving me a little piece of your home and life is really sweet and I am grateful to share this with you," she says, placing a hand on my arm big eyes looking up into mine.

Her beautiful, big eyes almost darkening to match the hot chocolate in her cup, still providing a warm welcome that pulls me closer, makes me want to share more with her every second.

I wake up, the room dark, an "are you still watching" message across the screen of her laptop and her head nestled onto my shoulder, arm and leg wrapped around me clinging like a koala. We must have fallen asleep shortly after putting our mugs down and curling up under the blanket. I smile down at her as I slowly move her leg, then her arm off of me, before sliding out from under her head, slowly and silently as not to wake her up. Once upright, I close and move her laptop to the desk in the guest room, plugging it in so that it's charged for her tomorrow.

I remember I haven't washed the mugs, and while I rinsed the pan it isn't clean and I don't want to leave her with a dirty kitchen; plus,

I could probably use some water. Once I make my way down the hallway to the kitchen I notice the time on the stove reads 3:34 a.m.

Well, I guess that's better than not sleeping at all.

I've always had difficulty sleeping, typically unable to fall asleep, and if I did fall asleep it was only for a few hours before waking up again, which is why working nights was always so easy for me.

"What are you doing?" I hear a quiet, sleepy voice from the hallway a few minutes later.

"Shit, Jules, I'm sorry. Did I wake you up? I was trying to be quiet." I put the pan in the drying wrack and dry my hands before walking toward her as she rubs her eyes.

"No, but I woke up and you weren't there," she says still half asleep.

I reach her placing my hands on her hips before pulling her into my chest.

"I woke up, and realized we fell asleep with the show playing, and without cleaning the dishes," I reply into the top of her head.

She turns her head to the side before yawning and saying, "So you got up to clean at 3:30 in the morning?"

"Yes," I reply, slightly embarrassed, but mostly sorry for waking her.

"You're so weird, Schmidty."

"I know. Come on, let's get you back to bed."

"Are you coming, too?"

"Do you want me to?"

"I want to be where you are," she says, wrapping her arms around my neck and presses the side of her face against my chest. I move my hands from her hips so I can princess carry her down the hall, back to her bedroom.

She falls asleep almost instantly, nestling against me before I even realize she's drifted off. One second, she's tucked against me, her fingers resting lightly against my chest, and the next her breathing goes soft and even.

I should try to sleep, too. God knows I need it. But I already know there is nothing that will still my mind now.

I stare at the ceiling, at the shadows of the ceiling fan rotating around and around. I try to focus on each rotation hoping to lull myself into a sleep. All I can think about is her, the way she laughed earlier, how her hair hangs around her face, how she closes her eyes when she's tipping her head back to laugh, the way her hands feel on my skin, her big espresso brown eyes lighting up at making homemade soup. But more importantly, the thing I can't get out of my brain is the way she looks at me like she sees something worth holding onto.

And that is the scariest of them all.

I've never felt this before. I have never felt this feeling in my chest. It's like a deep ache that runs through my muscles straight to my bones. It's not the kind of pull that sits heavy in your chest, but it does whisper *stay, don't let her go*.

But I have to. We said this was a one-time thing and that it couldn't be anything more. I mean, how could it be? I'll be on the other side of the country in a couple of days and then who knows where I'll end up. My life isn't stable, and her entire life is here in Fisher Creek.

And yet, lying here, I can't remember a single good reason why.

Other than Julie saying she doesn't want anything more, agreeing to keep this solely between us.

She moves in her sleep, slipping away from me, and I instinctively want to pull her close. Keep her here with me. Then it hits me like a ton of bricks. I can't stay.

Plus, if Noah gets home and I'm not at his house, I'll never hear the end of the interrogation.

I ease out from under her, careful not to wake her, and pull the blanket up to her shoulders. For a minute, I just stand there, watching her, memorizing everything about her but settling on the peace that emanates from her.

The ache in my chest deepens. Like there's a string attached to her from my chest that pulls tighter with every step, threatening to snap.

I find a notepad on the counter and a pen that barely works, and I scratch out a note:

You are the most amazing person I have ever met, Jules. Thank you for this weekend and for being a listening ear. I don't want this trip to end, but I fear I will never leave if I don't go now.

– Pretty Boy

I leave it on the counter, next to a mug and the homemade hot chocolate recipe before walking out the door. The door clicks behind me, a little too loud, and I cringe, hoping it doesn't wake her up. She's had a busy few days and needs her rest. The last thing I want is for her to burn out before she even gets started.

By the time I'm halfway back to Noah's, the sun's starting to rise, and already, I can't stop thinking about her—and I don't know I ever will.

10

1 Year Later

Morale is at an all-time low as we return, heads hung and skin caked in dirt. Today was a bad day; every day we lose someone is a bad day, but today felt exceptionally hard. I strip and step into the wooden shower, allowing the lukewarm water to cover my body, washing away any sand and grime left.

The water feels cool, over my heating body, as anger begins to boil within. We have lost too many people this week. Too many men, who won't have the opportunity to go home to their families. Whose families will have to mourn them without knowing the entirety of what happened.

There is an ache in my chest that will never go away after watching them load one of our own into that plane to be sent stateside, deceased.

I continue to scrub my skin raw, ensuring the sand is no longer stuck to me, while also trying to remove the pain from the loss. Not physical pain, the empty feeling that sits deep in my stomach.

But it doesn't leave.

Instead, it intensifies as I wonder, who would mourn me?

Who would they send my remains to?

Is there someone stateside who I want to know all the details?

And time and time again, the only person I can think of is Julie.

Julie Rowe.

It's been a full year since my trip to Fisher Creek and there hasn't been a day where she doesn't cross my mind at some point. I know she said we can't do this. A relationship is not feasible, being in different parts of the world, having different careers.

But she also offered to take some of the noise from me. Does that offer still stand?

I guess there's really only one way to find out.

I finish showering, dry off, and dress quickly before heading to the housing tent. I move the tan tent flap and am met with heavy air, the kind that takes your breath away and makes your stomach turn. Everyone is hurting today. Some heads are held up by their hands as they lean over onto their knees, while others are solemnly writing. Writing letters to their loved ones, presumably telling them, they love them and they wish to hold them a little tighter today.

Finding my cot, I sit on the edge, pulling out the pad of paper, and begin writing.

Jules,

I know we said it was one night only, and that it's been almost a year since our weekend together. But sometimes, it's really lonely out here; all the death and destruction are hard.

Don't get me wrong, there are a lot of good times, funny moments that I have with the unit, especially Kneland.

But when the day is dark, and the voices rise, I think of the person who is the embodiment of sunshine, who told me if I ever need to quiet the voices, this is where to go.

So after a year of fighting off the urge to write you, I'm giving in.

I don't really know where to go from here. What does one say to the beautiful girl they can't get out of their head in a letter? "I hope you're doing well," sounds too formal.

S,o J, tell me about Fisher Creek? About Creek and Kettle? Tell me one thing that makes you tick? Distract me from the wild, wild west of my brain as my pen pal. My cheesy pen pal who might be kind enough to send some pastries or coffee beans one of these days.

'Cause let me tell you one thing, I miss a good cup of coffee.

Anyway, I know it's not easy being friends with someone across the world who may not live to see tomorrow, so if you choose not to respond, I understand. No hard feelings.

But I truly hope you write back.

-Pretty Boy

I write and rewrite the letter repeatedly, trying to find the right words before settling on the final letter, knowing there would never be a perfect letter.

"Today sucks," I hear Kneland say, followed by a thump as he collapses onto his cot.

"Agreed," I reply.

"You're due for leave soon. Why don't you take it now?"

"Where would I go?" I ask.

He's right, I am due for leave, but in reality, I haven't even considered leave since the start of our deployment.

He shrugs in response.

"Schmidt!" I hear Commander Gibson call from the tent entrance.

"Yes, sir?" I reply, standing immediately.

"You're due for a leave. When do you want to take it?" he asks.

"I don't, sir."

"You don't?"

"I don't need it, sir. I am sharp and ready to keep going."

"It's not an option, Schmidt. You are required to take it. It doesn't matter where you go, but you need to take a leave. Need rest," he responds.

"Fine," I say, defeated, knowing I'm not going to win this battle. I might as well get it over with instead of fighting the inevitable.

"Great, next week you'll have four days," he says before walking away.

I turn annoyed to see Kneland smirking at me from his cot. He is such a damn know-it-all all and sometimes it's hard not to be irritated by him.

***

The car comes to a stop along the side of the big brick building, where the building stands out brightly against the sky, heavy with low gray clouds. I haven't told anyone where I'm going, wanting to surprise her, the moment of walking in and seeing her face light up. The other part just needed to know she could still be my anchor, keeping me sane and quiet when the noise was deafening.

Creek and Kettle is just as beautiful as the day I was here for the grand opening. The big picture window is spotless, giving way to the beauty that lies within. I pause outside the window, uniform jacket tugged tight against the chill, looking for a sign she was here. I scanned the room, looking for that silky raven hair and endless smile before I see her. Jules. Sitting at the counter, her dark hair falling forward as she leans close to a man I don't recognize. Not that I would, I'm not from here.

They're laughing, the kind of laugh that lives in the chest. Every muscle pulls taut as she touches the man's arm, casual and familiar, like she's done this more than once. My pulse echoes in my ears, and for a heartbeat, I think she'll turn and catch me standing here. I have to get out of here. I turn on my heels as quickly as possible, running back to the car before she can see me, standing here, speechless, stupidly heartbroken. We said we wouldn't get caught up in each other. That we couldn't be in a relationship. That was a one-weekend thing. But here I am, in a foreign town, pining and breaking over her.

The drive to the bed and breakfast feels endless, salt and sand crunching under the tires, the air feeling colder than before. I park the car, gather my bags, and start the short trek to the door when the first flakes begin to fall.

It's snowing. Of course it's snowing, I'm in Wisconsin after all. Tilting my head back, I let out a laugh that sounds more broken than amused, one that I hardly recognize, sharp, almost sinister.

I make it to the door before my stomach rumbles and I feel nauseous remembering the last time I walked through this door. Julie thrown over my shoulder, laughing, leading to the best night of my life.

I can't do this.

I turn, put my head down and trek back to my car, fighting the wind and snow as it picks up around me.

I don't know where I will go for the weekend but it can't be here.

I've been broken before, I'll pick myself up from this, and I refuse to let one small mishap ruin the rest of my leave.

I came to see her. Instead, I'll learn to let her go.

11

I walk into the rec tent that smells faintly of dust and instant coffee, the kind of scent that clings to everything but makes me miss good coffee more than a normal day. It always brings my mind back to Creek and Kettle, enjoying a latte and the smile on Julie's face, only to be further reminded that she has someone else in her life now, and it's time to let her go.

The generator hums outside, fighting to keep the TV alive, and Kneland's already sprawled on the beat-up couch like he owns the place.

"All right," he says, holding up two cases like they are sacred cassettes. "*Criminal Minds*, *Band of Brothers* or *The Office*?"

I snort. "You seriously want to watch a war show while we're in an actual war?"

"History, bro. Education." He grins, toothpick bouncing at the corner of his mouth. "Besides, I need to see guys with worse haircuts than ours."

"*Criminal Minds*," I shoot back. "I need something more messed up than the world we live in."

"You want to watch something more messed up than what we deal with daily?" he retorts, a bit of anxiety tied into his tone.

"Yeah, there's always something worse, right?"

"You ever watch shows with someone back home?" he asks, his voice lower now, more careful.

"Yeah," I say.

Julie's face flashes in my head, the night on her bed, the glow of a laptop between us, her smile as we watched some crazy reality TV show, soaking up all the meaningless drama between participants.

Kneland nods, eyes fixed on the floor. "Same. Ollie hates reality TV, preferring anything with crime in it. We binged *Criminal Minds* and *NCIS*. I'd pretend to hate it, but..." He shrugs, a crooked smile on his face. "She'd be so invested in the mystery and figuring out who the unsub was that I couldn't help but love every moment. She'd even nestle in close when something was particularly messed up or scary."

Silence settles in for a moment, broken only by the static hum of the generator. Then I let out a laugh, not a happy one, more like something caught between longing and regret. "It's crazy, isn't it? We're half a world away, arguing about what show to watch, when in reality, we're talking about the girls we left behind."

Kneland looks up, and for once, there's no smart-ass grin. Just understanding. "Guess that's the point, huh? They're with us. Even here. But I don't think I realized you had someone back home," he says, almost skeptical.

"I wouldn't say I have someone back home. It was a one-time thing, but she definitely created a core memory, one that I don't think I'll ever forget. But nothing like the love you and Ollie shared," I respond, the words escaping before I have a minute to realize what I've said. Hopefully bringing his attention back to him.

"Oh," is all he replies, followed by a long moment of silence. He drops his head back to the floor before sitting up and placing his elbows on his knees, clearly deep in thought.

"What's going on, man?" I ask.

"It's just Ollie," he says, his voice breaking a little bit. "I can't help but wonder if I really fucked up. I miss her, man. And it's not just the idea of having her, I miss the way she looked at me and smiled, always proud of whatever I did. The way her body fit perfectly with mine. Her sense of humor, which always made me laugh, even when everything around me was dark. She was a light, man. The light of my freaking life, and I ended it."

"Have you thought about reaching out?" I ask, sitting next to him.

"What would I say? Shit, Ollie, I messed up. Breaking up with you was the worst decision of my life, and I regret it every day," he says, almost desperately.

"I mean, yeah. What is the worst thing that can happen? She tells you to fuck off? Great, we're right where we are right now, but at least we'd know she's not sitting in Wisconsin waiting for you," I reply.

"She's still in school...I can't risk her giving up her dream for me. We're set to be over here for the next four years. I can't ruin her life, plus, she already hates me. You saw how her brother reacted."

"Yeah, less than a week after you ended things with his sister. Of course, he was angry. Kneland, I love you, you're the brother I never had. But you don't know that she would've given up everything. You both deserve happiness, so tell her how you feel. There's no guarantee for tomorrow. We lose too many men here every day to not tell our loved ones how we feel," I say.

"Yeah, yeah. I know you're right, but I don't like it."

I nod and press play on *The Office*. As the theme song blares through the old speakers, I realize the debate is less about what to watch, but more about who we are when we aren't in uniform, or who we want to be when this is over.

Kneland has always been more than the guy in the bunk next to me, but in this moment, he's become my brother.

"Fine. We'll watch *The Office* for the stupid jokes. But you owe me," I say.

"Kneland, Schmidt," I hear Hayes call from outside the tent.

"Rec tent," I call back.

"Mail," he responds, moving the tent flap. Hayes is one of the newer guys in our unit, taking the place of a man who lost his life a few weeks back. He's shorter than us with short blond hair, easily hidden by his cap. His bright blue eyes stand out against his abnormally pale skin, not accustomed to the constant heat of the blaring desert sun. Hayes still has a hopeful innocence about him, coupled with excitement for his first deployment, which is almost heartwarming, and part of me hopes that innocence is able to stick with him for a while.

He hands Noah the small stack he typically receives from his mother and sister. Sometimes there's a happy birthday or holiday card from Olivia, but neither are close, so I can't imagine there being something like that today.

Hayes carries a small box with a letter taped to the top of it that he stretches out to me. I pause, confused for a moment, having never received mail, let alone a package, since starting our most recent deployment. Hell, the only person I've written to is J, and that was months ago. I can't imagine she would reply now.

I slowly take the package from him, noticing the lack of a return address on it.

"Thank you, Hayes," I say, hopefully dismissing him from the moment.

Ripping open the end of the envelope, there's a flutter in my stomach, hoping it is Julie.

Pretty Boy,

I'm sorry it took so long for me to write you back. The truth is, I wasn't going to. I sat down many times, weighing the pros and cons of writing you. But in the end, the pros outweigh the cons, and the only con was tied to fear. I have never been someone to bow to my fear, so why would I start now?

Creek & Kettle is good; it has been steady, we are about to start tourist season again, and if it is anything like the last one, I am going to have to hire more help.

I truthfully cannot begin to imagine what the day-to-day looks like for you. The pain, the death, and the destruction must be impossibly hard to deal with. But for me, when things are hard, I focus on something good in my life or a happy memory that will make me smile. Like that goofy smile where you think everyone around you thinks you're crazy.

I'll let you in on a little secret: my memory is the day we went sledding and watched Survivor with hot chocolate.

As for your final question, things that make me tick. I don't know if I have something that particularly makes me tick, but something that really irritates me is when people don't have access to a good cup of coffee. How do you get up in the morning?

-J

The smile that emerges on my face must be one of those goofy ones that she mentioned because Kneland and Hayes are both looking at me with a confused look.

"You smile?" Hayes asks, breaking into a friendly smile.

Noah elbows him in the side. "Who's making you smile like that? You never get mail," he asks.

I immediately freeze up, not wanting to tell him it's Julie from his hometown, because I think he'd probably kill me. One, because I didn't tell him, but two, he is from a small town and their family is close.

"Oh, just someone I met on my leave, we decided to be pen pals."

"Pen pals, huh?" Noah asks, squinting his eyes.

"Yes, Kneland. I'm married to the army; there is no time for a relationship in my life. You know this."

"Okay, okay, but what's in the package?" Hayes asks.

I forgot the package was even sitting on my lap after reading her letter, heart racing.

The box is small, taped to hell, corners dented from the journey to get here. I take my time opening it, trying to gently rip the packing tape before finally grabbing a pen and stabbing it into the crease, slicing it open.

I smell it, immediately. Coffee. Real coffee. Rich, dark, nothing like the thin, bitter stuff we choke down every morning. She actually sent me a package of coffee grounds. The same coffee grounds she uses in her shop every day.

I can't stop smiling. It just happens, slow and stupid, because I know exactly what it took to get here. Julie thought about me, *really* thought, and the thought of that feels heavy. It's been a long time since someone has considered me and done something so kind.

Hayes whistles. "You've gotta be kidding. That's actual coffee?"

Kneland leans over next to me, eyes wide. "Man, you just hit the literal jackpot." My heart rate accelerates, slight panic that he would recognize the packaging on the coffee sample, but he seems to have already moved on to making a pot.

They're already talking about brewing it, laughing and arguing over who gets the first cup because anything is better than the hot water with a hint of coffee in it that we have. I let them. But I just sit there for a second, running my thumb over the bag, breathing it in.

To them, it's caffeine.

To me, it's a reminder of the one person who is ingrained into not only my head, but my heart and soul.

12

4 Years Later

I have always hated mail days. They are like a constant punch in the chest, and when you finally catch your breath again, boom, another hit. Not only do I get to see everyone around me receive letters from their loved ones, but I always end up with this pit-of-the-stomach feeling of hope that Julie might write me another letter. I know it was only one night. One night with this beautiful, amazing girl who was a breath of fresh air, the rainbow after a thunderstorm, and my brain chemistry is forever altered. After the first letter, I hoped she would continue to write, but all I have received is radio silence.

She's all I think about when I wake up, when I go to sleep, and everything in between. The only thing I know to do to clear my head is go to the gym, and there is only so much iron I can pick up and put down.

But she's always there.

"Schmidty!" I hear Noah yell from the front of the community tent.

Turning, I see him coming with multiple letters in his hand. I swear, this is the most loved man I've ever met—his family never misses a mail day. But I also know Noah has gotten good at masking his true feelings.

After things with Ollie collapsed, I know he secretly hopes every letter, phone call, or text message is from her. He misses her more than he is probably willing to admit. In his head, he thinks he did the right thing to protect her, but his heart is fighting to get her back, to love her always, and you'll never out-fight your heart; it's only a matter of time.

"Bro, did you not hear me call you? You have mail," Noah says as he approaches where I'm sitting at a table in the common area. I don't usually hang out in the community lounge, but anything to get out of the sun today, it's hotter than a hand grenade and ready to boil us from the inside out.

My body freezes at his statement when it finally registers in my brain.

I. Have. Mail.

Sweat starts to drip down the back of my neck, and I feel as if I'm going to vomit. Who sent the mail? Is it from Julie? I haven't heard anything from her in years, even after I wrote to tell her where to send letters during our long-term assignment. She told me not to fall in love with her, and I didn't, but she was the first person I ever felt completely comfortable with, and I knew I could be myself with her. The first person who saw me as Jarred Schmidt, not the kid abandoned by his parents, the unlovable one, or even the army kid. I was just Jarred.

"From who?" I ask skeptically.

"It's a federal offense to open someone else's mail, Schmidt, you know this."

"Just give it to me."

He hands me the envelope, and my stomach bottoms out. The return address is from James A. Schmidt—my father. My biological father. The piece of shit who abandoned me when I was seven years old because I was too complicated of a child, and heroin was more important.

What. The. Actual. Fuck?

A large part of me wants to just rip the entire thing into shreds and bury it, but there's a nagging part of me deep down that has to know what he could possibly want now. After all of these years of silence. My guess—*money*.

"You don't have to read it."

"I do, after all these years, I *have* to know why he's reaching out now."

"Do you want me to stay?"

"I don't care," I respond with more bite than intended. "Sorry, yeah, you can stay."

Noah sits across from me in silence, opening his letters as I slowly rip the end of the envelope to take the letter out.

My boy,

I've started this letter over and over again, and each time the words don't come out right. I don't think they ever will, but I have to at least try.

I'm writing to you not as the man who raised you, but as the man who's finally been trying to make things right, and as a father trying to make things right before it's too late. There is nothing I can say that will truly explain our actions. They will not erase the pain we caused you as a child, but I would like the opportunity to explain everything.

We left you because we were sick. We are sick. We have a disease. Addiction. We have been battling our disease since the moment we left you. I didn't understand and didn't know how to survive outside of it. We let it swallow us whole, and let it steal us from you.

I have been sober for ten years now, fighting every day to be better, not just for you but for Sophie, your sister. She just turned seven, her birthday was last week. She looks just like you, smart as a whip, curious about everything. Even you. She knows she has a big brother serving our country. She asks about you, especially wants to know when she can meet you.

Your mother got help too, she struggles more with her battle relapsing after giving birth to Soph, but has been fighting every day. I know she regrets leaving you every day. Sometimes I still catch her crying into one of your old blankets.

We were weak and scared. And instead of being the parents you deserved, we fled. And that is something that I'll regret until the day I die, which actually isn't going to be too far from now. My liver is failing, they say, from the years of abuse. I have less than a year to live. And while I'm not afraid of dying, I am afraid of not making amends with you.

I know I don't deserve forgiveness, I'm not even sure if I deserve to write this letter, but you need to know, I have thought about writing you every day that I have been sober. You didn't deserve the absence, no child does. I can't go back in time and change the past. Trust me, I would. But I can tell you that leaving this world without writing you causes unbearable pain deep in my heart.

I can only hope that you have it in your heart to forgive not only me but your mother as well. Please know that we are sorry for the pain and heartache we have caused you. If you ever want to visit, talk, or have questions, I'll be here, ready to answer. And if you choose to never respond, I'll understand. I'll still love you. I have never stopped loving you. Always have. Always will.

-Dad

I burst out laughing upon finishing the letter. But not the *ha-ha, that's a funny story* laugh. The type of deep, almost maniacal, laugh that happens when you're so angry you don't know how to respond. *I'll still love you. I have never stopped loving you.* Bull-fucking-shit.

That man never loved me a day in his life. And he wants my forgiveness now? Why? Because he's is dying?

He didn't write that letter out of the goodness of his heart. He wrote it for his benefit so he can feel better about his pathetic excuse of parenting.

"Hey, you okay?" Noah asks. I almost forgot that he was sitting here with me.

"Yeah, it's just my shitty dad trying to make amends before he dies. Turns out, he's capable of love, just not me. I have a seven-year-old sister," I reply, hands shaking. My stomach is in my chest. Mind racing.

What about me is so unlovable?

Why were they able to get clean for Sophie but not me?

Why can they love her and provide her a life but couldn't for me?

What is wrong with me?

"Fuck, dude, that's rough. I'm sorry. I know it doesn't change anything but they don't deserve you," Noah replies, looking shell-shocked at the news I just received.

"Thanks, man," I say, getting up from the table. "I'm going to hit the gym to burn off some steam."

"Want me to come with you? I can always use an extra workout."

"Nah, I'm good," I say, forcing a small smile at him. I'm anything but good, and he knows that. But I need to spend some time alone to work through my thoughts.

He nods, and that's all the approval I need to grab my things and walk out of the humid sticky tent. I don't bother taking off my boots, change into sneakers, or even athletic gear. Just throw my pack, letters, and all onto the cot, then head straight to the gym tent. The door flaps are taped open and held in place with sandbags to allow airflow, mainly to keep the stench down. We all come to for some "iron therapy" after a tough day or week, often without saying a word to another, acknowledging that we all have some ghosts who live with us here.

The smell of sweat, metal, and dirty rubber gives almost a sense of welcoming to the gym, knowing that while we don't talk about feelings or emotions, we are likely all feeling the same ones. And are not alone.

Half the guys here are running to burn off some steam. But not me, I detest running. If I'm running, there better be a snack at the finish line, or something is chasing me. Instead, I chalk up and get under the only bar available, ready for the pain. I want it heavy, I want to feel my muscles shaking under me, feel as if my legs can't carry me back to my cot. I want to be so exhausted that I can finally drift into a night-long sleep.

The one constant out here is the bar isn't going to ask questions. The weight isn't going to care if I'm worthy or loveable. It doesn't care what's happening in the real world, who is okay, who made it, and who is falling apart.

One rep. Two. My legs shake at five, and I know this will be the strip set from hell.

The strip set that will entirely clear my thoughts, I just need to push through it.

Eventually, I stop thinking. About how tired I am. About the anger and the letter I received. The burn is the only thing true, honest, and in that moment that's all I need.

I don't understand how my father could think, after all these years, I would want to hear from him. That I would want to know they were able to get clean for another child and love her for the last seven years but couldn't be bothered to reach out sooner. And all while I'm drowning in my emotional trauma, feelings, and throwing this weight around, there is a blur of memory, of comfort from a friend that I crave, now more than ever.

Julie.

Julianna Catherine Rowe.

After doing the strip set from hell of deadlifts, I all but collapse on the floor, reaching for water bottle when a familiar, caring voice comes from behind me.

"Twenty years later and James finally reaches out."

Gibson. The only man who truly knows about my father. The abandonment, the years of therapy.

"How'd you know?" I ask between sips.

"All the mail comes to me and I distribute it out as necessary, I saw his name and figured I'd probably find you here."

"Why now?" I ask "It's been forever and I've finally gotten to a good place, what does he want now?"

"I don't know, kid, sometimes people do things for their own benefits. Others, they truly mean their words. Maybe he really has changed and wants to make amends. Maybe he just wants to clear his conscious. But you'll never know if you don't reply," he says sitting down next to me.

"I don't know what I want to do. I want to tell him to fuck off. Too little, too late. But there's another kid involved now. I need to know she's safe and loved. But right now, I'm too angry to care, too angry to feel anything but resentment toward them all, and that isn't fair. She's just a kid." My voice begins to crack, years of trauma coming to the surface that I try to stuff back down—as deep as it'll go. The noise is loud. Too loud.

"Write the letter, say everything you're thinking and feeling right now. Don't send it, but reread it in a week, and see if you still feel the same way. If you do, then you know that's what you really mean, and send it. And if it's not, then don't send it. Who cares? No one will know," Gibson says.

"When did you get so wise, Gibby?" I say, knocking a shoulder into him. I have been insanely fortunate to have grown with him since high school, and be in his unit my entire military career. He's been more of a father figure to my then my own dad ever would be, which also means I take every opportunity I can to mess with him, like calling him Gibby.

Watch it, partner, or you'll be rucking for days." He laughs back at me.

I rile back in fake horror before replying, "I don't even know if I can stand after all the deadlifts, let alone do a burpee."

"Come on, Schmidt, let's get you up so you can go get your beauty sleep," he says, helping me off the dirt floor.

"Thanks for the help, sir. I think I'm going to write that letter first," I say, walking out of the gym tent, working my way back to the bunks.

Sitting on the edge of my bunk, paper in one hand, pen in another, and a pile of crumpled up scraps at my feet, I know this isn't going the way I want it to. The words aren't coming to me the way I had hoped. The noise is too loud, too chaotic.

If you ever need a person to take some of the noise, I'm your girl. We'll call it pen pals, rings over and over inside my head. I haven't tried writing Julie in four years, I have no idea if she'll even remember me or still be a part of this. But I have to try.

Taking a deep breath, I let it all out and begin to write and write and write. Just not the letter I thought I was writing tonight.

13

1 YEAR LATER

I used to hate mail days, now I find myself jumping up in the morning waiting for them to come, like what I imagine a kid does on Christmas morning, except it's actually like 3 a.m. and their parents literally just went to bed.

Yeah, that's definitely me.

Julie and I have been writing back and forth for almost a year now and she has become more than just a pen pal. Julie is my best friend, just don't tell Noah. Her selflessness and kindness is unparalleled, taking leftover goods from her coffee shop to the homeless and veterans, hanging local artists' work on the walls of the shop for sale. Everything she does is for everyone else, including me.

9/15

Schmidt,

I know it has been some time since we have written. Life has been crazy here, the store is busy and I've had to hire additional help just to get through the general days. The truth is, I'm scared. Scared that writing again will open a door I don't know if I can step through. Scared of the feelings this friendship might stir up. You've always had a way of making things feel real, and real can be overwhelming sometimes.

But then I read what you shared about your dad's letter, and it hit me like a punch in the chest. I could feel the weight behind your words, the silence between the lines. I realized this wasn't just about me being afraid. It was about the overwhelming noise you are experiencing. So here I am, finally writing. I know I can't fix anything or make it all go away, but if I can be the voice that takes some of the noise out of your head, even if just for as long as it takes you to read this letter.

So, pretty boy, let some of that noise go, give it to me. Let's make this pen pal thing something we'll never forget.

-Jules

Her letter broke my heart; I knew telling her about my dad's letter would be hard to read. But it I think it would truly be hard for anyone to read. Even though the idea of this friendship was scary, she reached out. Reached her hand out to support someone thousands of miles away. I was so relieved when she wrote back that I started to cry before immediately responding.

9/15

Jules,

I'm so glad you wrote back, even though this friendship is scary. I think about our night a lot, especially when the noise is loud, which is often. Especially after that letter. I can't wrap my head around the fact that I have a little sister and that she is loved. I know they have a disease, and I can't fault them about it. But why couldn't they love me? Did I do something as a child to make them stop loving me?

How is FC? I feel like so much time has passed and I'm missing such a large part of your life. I want to know everything, and I have too many questions to fit on this sheet of paper.

Thanks for writing back, J. You made such a difference in my day.

-Pretty boy

10/15

Schmidt,

Also, I am done being sad for you and am now just going to be angry for you. THAT BASTARD. Who does he think he is that he can just show up out of nowhere and try to make amends with you? I'm so sorry that he made you feel unloved, because I can assure you that is not true in the slightest. Are you going to respond to him? What about your sister?

I get what you mean about missing everything. I can't even begin to fathom all the things you have been through over there. FC is amazing, just had a full year of really successful business partnerships with local businesses, and went to celebrate. Thought of you when Cole started to sing karaoke.

-J

Sometimes letters came weekly, and others they took over a month. Life's busy for the two of us so we developed a system that she called the blink system. Two characters in a book she loved used to tell if the other was okay, only for us it's stars at the top of the letter. Five stars—amazing, three stars—we had a rough day, and one star—need someone. She said we couldn't have five stars be bad because that's the highest rating a book can get and we would be disrespecting the system by changing it.

I saw myself changing, changing the way I thought about love and the important people in my life. There was more than one occasion where I saw the people around me changing, too. Some for the better, others for the worst, facial lines hardened with every loss. Every soldier who didn't make it home. How we responded to those loses, everything was changing.

Noah, in particular, was changing from the golden retriever, loving best friend I've had for the last decade and is now becoming worn, harder with sharper edges. Constantly checking for letters or messages from who I can only assume is Olivia. He still hasn't gotten past that relationship, and I don't think he ever will. Before graduation, he had his life planned out for him. A white picket fence, a dog, a few kids. Living the American Dream.

My dream is to survive. Make a difference in my community and survive, I don't need to live. I need to survive. But now I'm craving more and he was craving less.

I watch my best friend's dream slowly become a dream I never thought I deserved, never truly wanted, but now when I close my eyes at night, I see the small streets of Fisher Creek, standing on a ladder, against the wall at Creek and Kettle, hanging a local artisan's piece on the wall. Climbing down to see a beautiful raven-haired girl waiting to kiss me on the cheek as we finish the day.

And in this moment, I know I need to make a change, a drastic change right now. I can't let my best friend throw his life away for this career, we see too much death every day for that.

So I march over to Commander Gibson's tent and say, "I need to write new letters. Last letters, to be specific."

14

4 Years Later

"Come on, one drink," Kneland pleads as we plop onto our cots, prepping for the weekend off. We're fortunate to have some off time each month in which we're able to go into town, explore, or just relax. More often than not, we hang out around base, working out or catching up on sleep.

"Fine, one drink, but only if we can find a dive bar. No clubbing," I say, pulling off my boots to change into jeans.

He throws his head back, pumping his fist into the air celebrating his win. The pure, unfiltered joy radiating from his pores is contagious, causing a smile and small laugh to slip from me.

***

The bar is tucked down a dark, narrow alley with a small, half-lit neon sign outside that simply says Bar. As we approach, the music—or I guess, it's more static—becomes louder alongside the conversations between patrons.

Perfect. This is perfect. It will be a quaint, quiet night out.

The door opens and an overwhelming stench of stale cigarettes wafts out. Walking inside, it's obvious the thick smell is baked into the walls, posters, and air. The bartender has a cigarette glued to his lips, while two men at the bar playing cards are each holding one between two fingers. Arguing over who won.

We walk up to the bar and flag down the bartender for beers before turning to find a place to sit. I always prefer the far corner booth to see everything going on around, but Noah likes to be in the center of room, especially when he is missing Olivia. He will drown his thoughts in anyone around him, entertain them, and then never go home with them to avoid the guilt gnawing at his soul. I wish this man would just freaking talk to her about everything—it's eating him alive and won't get better until he finds closure. Hell, it's been at least 8 years already. Not that texting her on her birthday or every major holiday will get him that closure. I roll my eyes to myself just thinking about it.

There's plenty of space, a group of girls sitting in the far corner, some locals playing darts at the other end, then the two arguing souls at the front. Still arguing. We settle for a small bar top table in the middle, perfectly centered between the bar and the music speaker, making it almost impossible to hear anything around us through the half music, half static nonsense that was playing.

I'm just taking a sip of my drink when two girls walk up to us to strike up conversation. One is tall and thin, with dark brown hair and deep tan skin that has golden undertones. The other is shorter, more athletically built, with equally tan skin, but her hair is more of a chestnut color. Noah instantly perks up at the shorter one—Georgia, I think she said her name is. When she asks if she can sit with us, I smile and nod at her and her friend, Jasmine.

I really wish this wasn't happening. I just wanted a quiet drink with my best friend, who needs a night out.

We lost someone in our unit this week, and it weighs on each of us a little differently. The noise in my head is blaming me for not being alert enough when patrolling or responding fast enough the gunfire. The investigation says there was nothing I could've done differently to change the outcome. It was just a wrong place, wrong time type of situation. The worst.

Julie's latest letter cheered me up a bit today, as I was able to read it before Kneland barged in, begging me to go out.

Schmidty,

Your last letter had two stars, I hope everything's okay, or at least turning in the right direction. Please let me know if there is anything I can do to help. Maybe I will send over some of Bec's world famous cookies for you guys with my next letter. Just don't tell Kneland they're Bec's. I'm not going to lie, I've missed you a bunch these last few months and was thinking maybe we should try to plan a time to get together on your next leave.

Always here pen pal,

-J

Smack.

I'm brought back to reality by the sound a large smack onto the wooden bar table. Noah's head is smashed against it by one of the random guys from the far side of the bar. When did he even go over here? The girls shriek and back away behind me.

"Whoa," I say, "What is going on here? We're just having a drink. He didn't do anything." I remain calm, trying to defuse the situation. Noah elbows the guy in the stomach, causing him to release his head and allowing him to stand upright.

"This prick was all over my woman," the guy says, recovering from the blow.

"*Your* woman?" I hear a small voice from behind me. "I haven't been your woman since you gave me a black eye," she says, standing her ground.

Noah's face blanches, knowing the trigger that was just pulled.

"Excuse me? This man gave you a black eye, and is still breathing?" I grit out, looking at Georgia.

"Apparently," she says with a shrug.

"Schmidt," Noah says with warning laced into his voice. "Back down."

I stand there, blood boiling beneath me.

"Yeah, Schmidt, back down, and give my whore back to me"

"Oh for fuck's sake," Noah says.

"The only thing I'm giving back to you is your teeth, after I knock them out of your head." And that's the last thing I say before all hell breaks loose, and I'm never allowed back in this bar again.

***

"I need to leave," I say, throwing the tent flap out of the way, as I walk—well, storm—into Commander Gibson's tent.

"Hi, Schmidt," he says, looking up from the table.

The sweat rolls off my forehead, with a well of emotions that I don't even know how to describe. Am I angry that she hit on me? Or that the jackass at the bar was rude to his girlfriend? Am I sad and lonely? What is this pitting feeling I have deep in my stomach? When did it start? Why is it here?

"Care to explain what's going on? Why are you sweating so much in the middle of the night?"

"I need to take a leave. I have this empty feeling deep inside me, and I need to figure out what is going on so that it doesn't affect my work."

"Does this have anything to do with what happened at the bar?" he asks, as if he was expecting this.

How does he—

Fucking Kneland.

Noah has always been able to tell when something's wrong and what will trigger me. He must've came here first instead of going to the shower hut when we got back.

"No. Maybe. I don't know." Which isn't a lie, because I don't exactly know what's happening right now.

"Kneland mentioned you were approached at the bar tonight, potentially asked to go spend the night with a beautiful woman, turned her down, and then completely shut down the rest of the night. I also know you've been receiving letters from one special J. Rowe." He stops, leaving an inflection in the statement, so it feels open-ended.

I look at him. And he looks back at me, as if he is waiting for me to reply.

Jules and I promised to keep this between us—whatever this is, our friendship. She's friends with Olivia, and now works closely with Bec, Kneland's sister. She doesn't want it to appear like we're picking sides or being bad friends to each other. Thus, our friendship is a secret and will always be a secret. The pain in my chest deepens at that thought. Maybe this feeling in my chest is related to the letters to Julie. Hell, maybe Jules is the cause of this.

"We're just pen pals. And I promised her no one would know," I whisper, looking around the tent to ensure there is no one else around.

"When did you start feeling this way?"

"The gnawing in my stomach? I don't know...tonight, I guess."

"After you were approached at the bar?"

"I guess?"

"When did you get the last letter?"

"This morning. It was mail day, Gibson, you know this—you handed it to me." I'm starting to get annoyed with his questioning. I just need him to approve this leave.

"Hmm. And where are you going to go for leave?"

"I haven't thought that far ahead."

"Could it have occurred to you that you want to go see Miss Rowe?"

Could it have occurred to me? *Yes.* Did it? *No.* Do I want to see Julie? *Abso-fucking-lutely.*

Shit.

"I have to go to Wisconsin, sir."

A soft and low warm laugh, laced with satisfaction and amusement, escapes Commander Gibson. "Five days. Starting now. Go," he says, not even looking up his desk.

"Yes, sir. Thank you, sir," I respond before making a beeline for the door. I don't even have a plane ticket or a bag packed, but those are all things I'll figure out on the way. I need to get out of here before he changes his mind.

"And, kid, figure out how you feel and tell her," I hear him yell over my shoulder.

***

The plane jolts as the wheels bounce off the tarmac upon landing. What's only a two-and-a-half hour flight from Boston to Milwaukee felt like an eternity, probably from the lack of sleep over the last forty-eight hours.

Being reminded of my past always brings my heart closer to home. The home I've built for myself but haven't actually accepted. I may have grown up in Louisiana with parents who was incapable of love and caring for a child, but my home is where my heart is, and it's constantly wondering back to Fisher Creek, Wisconsin.

Home of my best friend.

Well, I guess, home of my two best friends. Except one is still stuck in the desert while I'm standing in the summer sunshine outside the Milwaukee airport.

Squinting to keep the sun from burning my sleepy eyes, I look to find the closest rental place.

I probably should have thought this through before telling Gibson I needed leave immediately and jumping on the first plane back to the States, back to her.

"We only have a Toyota Camry left, sir," the gentleman with graying hair behind the counter says to me, as if I have an opinion in the car I drive.

"That's fine," I say, tapping my card on the counter subconsciously in anticipation of getting this car and starting to drive. If my memory serves me right, there is a two-hour drive out of the city, following the winding two-lane, tree-lined road back to the town that makes me feel at ease.

The only place in the entire world where the endless noise in my brain—the static that feels like it never shuts off, that I have learned to live with—finally shuts off.

There's a mumble that my brain tries to process through the static and inner monologue in my brain.

"Sir?"

Shit, what did he say? I need to get my head on straight if I'm going to make this work.

"Sorry, what was that?"

"Go through these doors on the left and the spot marked C32 is yours."

"Got it, thank you," I say, giving him a soft smile to show my gratitude.

The silver Toyota Camry is small, and my legs are cramped up toward my chest dropping into the driver's seat. This is going to be a long drive if I cannot figure out how to move the damn seat back. Climbing out of the car I drop onto the cement floor of the parking garage and try to examine the slightly worn black plastic and cloth for the lever.

Rushing to get to Fisher Creek as quickly as possible I pull the level and the seat slides all the back taking me with it.

"Shit." My shoulder hits the car door frame and I'm confident that will leave a mark, but it doesn't matter. What matters is that I get to Creek and Kettle before they close.

I think I must black out for the entire drive. The type of drive that, when I pull into the small parking lot near Creek and Kettle, I have no idea how I got here or made it here alive.

The white oak wood is bordered by stunning red brick both exteriorly and interiorly, making it nearly impossible to stop just inside the door to take everything in. The ding of the door chimes as I open the antique wooden door of Creek and Kettle, sending my heart lurching into my stomach. It's been almost seven years since I've been back in Wisconsin and nine since seeing Julie in person.

She may not even want to see me.

Will she even recognize me?

The same questions continue to march through my consciousness on repeat until I hear a familiar, warm and welcoming voice say, "You can have a seat wherever you'd like and I'll be right with you."

Turning toward the counter, I see a wave of raven hair tied up into a slick back high pony, and my heart rate accelerates at seeing her. She looks stunning in a white blouse and a flowy black skirt, head down, focusing on the foam art she's designing on a latte.

She hasn't noticed me yet, so I say, "Thank you," before finding a small two-person table against the wall where I can see the entire shop and Jules while she works.

Not long after, Julie finishes her latte art and hands the mug to the young woman, smiling and grabbing a menu before rounding the counter to look for her newest patron. Her coffee brown eyes widen as they land on me. Her body freezes, mouth parts slightly, eyebrows lift, and her expression shifting from relaxed to surprised or terrified. I'm hoping for the first.

I give a small smile and mouth, *hi,* across the busy café.

The café she owns has been transformed into a beautiful oasis for locals and tourists. It gives this warm, homey feeling of a local coffee shop where only the locals would go while also being modern and industrial enough to be a hit with all of the tourists that come into the small town to escape the summer heat.

"Schmidt?" she whispers when she gets to my table.

"Hi, Jules," I say, standing up to be closer to her as her eyes water slightly.

"What are you doing here?" she says into my chest when I pull her in for a hug.

"Here? Hoping to get some coffee."

She slaps me in the chest with the paper menu before wiping a tear before it can fall from her face. "Not the coffee shop, you buffoon. In Fisher Creek. Why are you here in Fisher Creek? Did something happen to Kneland?" Her expression changed again into utter worry.

"Wow, I see where I rank. No, J, Kneland is fine."

Not letting go of her, but stepping back slightly so I can look into her eyes, just in time for her to roll them at me.

"I had to see you, Jules. That's why I'm here."

She's unable to contain the tears any longer as they gently start to slide down her pink cheek.

"I'm sorry. I didn't mean to upset you. Please don't cry. I can go. I should've told you I was coming."

"No. It's just that you're here. In Fisher Creek. For me." She sniffles. "And Cassidy called out today, so I have to stay at the shop until close at three. And then all the closing duties. I can't even spend the day with you."

"Oh, honey," I say, bringing my thumb up to wipe away the tears. "That's okay, I brought a book, I'm perfectly happy buying every pastry and coffee in this fine establishment until I can have you in my arms again tonight."

"You're sure?"

I tap the book I placed on the table and nod.

"Positive." I smile at her. "Now, wipe those tears and get back to work. We can't have everyone think you've lost your hard edge."

She turns quickly on her heel, heading back toward the light brown counter against the wall opposite me, smiling and saying hello to each customer as she passes.

Seeing her in this element is like looking back in time while she was at FishyBar, working in her parents' business, full of energy and spunk. Only this time, it's her business and it's clear how much effort and love she has poured into Creek and Kettle. She's building more than just a business; she's building a sanctuary. The wall behind the counter is sand-colored shiplap, accenting the red brick wall in the front of the building perfectly, has many different frames of various artwork hanging on it. There doesn't appear to be any rhyme or reason associated with the artwork, no pattern in design, medium, or really anything, other than they are framed on the wall.

Upon closer look, I see all of the paintings or sketches are different from five years ago and take a minute to look at the new pieces for sale. My eyes fall on this beautiful winter painting of a lake and a couple having a snowball fight. My face begins to ache from smiling, as I remember back to the first night we spent together, in the snow at the bed and breakfast.

This beautiful place for the locals to feel at home, share their own businesses and showcase any work they have. And for the tourists, this is like a goldmine. A small business they can support, with the opportunity to support other local artisans, get coffee, and have access to the internet.

Really, the setup here is genius, and Julie is so sweet and personable that even when she's running around, she'll gives you a smile, make eye contact and talks to everyone. Her superpower is that she makes you feel like time has slowed, like you're the only person in a crowded room.

With a gentle clink, there's an iced latte and a crumbly loaf sitting on the table.

"Iced latte with a hint of vanilla and oat milk, and a cranberry lemon crumble cake made with products from the Bennett farm."

"I didn't even order yet," I say, raising an eyebrow toward her.

"You mentioned once that you miss 'good coffee, iced latte with a hint of vanilla' instead of the crap quality regular cream and sugar shit you're used to. So I figured this was the best place to start. Plus, you look like you could use some caffeine."

"You remember my coffee order?"

"Oh, Schmidty," she says with a hint of sarcasm in her voice. "I remember everything."

Me too, Jules. Me too.

Chapter 15

The clang of the blue open and closed sign being switched to closed brings my attention back to Creek and Kettle, and is music to my ears. I've only been sitting in this shop for about three hours, but it feels like an utter eternity.

Watching Julie work, or rather, trying not to watch her work, is like watching a couple dancing in public—mesmerizing and impossible to take your eyes off. Seeing Jules in her element is like that. I tried to keep my eyes and mind on the book I'm reading, but let's face it, I read maybe five pages.

She flips the sign to *Closed,* and I see the full release in her body—her job is demanding, having to be on all the time. And all I want to do is wrap her in my arms and worship her until all her stress and tension is gone.

Turning toward me, the mischievous smile I love spreads wide across her face, and she runs and leaps into my arms, wrapping her arms tightly around my neck and her legs around my waist, knocking me off balance.

"Whoa," I say, stabilizing her against me with one hand and catching us with the other.

"I can't believe you're here...like, actually here, in Fisher Creek. I didn't think I'd ever see you again," she says, squeezing tighter and resting her head against my shoulder.

"I couldn't go forever without seeing you," I say, returning her squeeze.

Putting her down, I grab her hand, not ready to let go of her touch yet, when the song on the radio changes. It's a country song, like the first time I was in Fisher Creek.

"Oh my god," she exclaims, squeezing my forearms with excitement. "We have to dance to this!"

"We do?"

"Jarred, this song is iconic. It's also the song we heard Parker sing at karaoke the night we met."

"You remember that?" I say, pausing and listening for a second.

"I already told you, I remember *everything*," she says with a nervous laugh, almost embarrassed.

"Me too," I whisper into her ear before kissing her soft, pale neck, just below the ear.

She smells like espresso and cinnamon—warm, spicy, and welcoming. Like curling up in a blanket after a long day in the rain.

"C'mon, no one is here, what's one dance?" She laughs nervously, but warm like the light orange lights casting halos along the old wooden floor.

"One dance, one rule?" I ask beginning us back to that night nine years ago.

"Just don't fall in love with me, Schmidt." She smirks, leaning into me.

Wrapping my arms around her, I pull her close, with one hand tight around the small of her back, the other interlacing between her fingers, we begin swaying back and forth in lazy circles around the shop. She rests her cheek against my chest and begins humming softly to the lyrics.

Everything else in the world becomes slowed, as if time stands, still just feeling our heartbeats together, as one.

Wanting to hear her giggle and laughter, I release my hand from her waist and raise our interlaced hands above our heads, preparing to spin her and maybe add a romantic dip. Her laughter erupts around us, light and bubbly, like the fizz of champagne, full of joy and affection.

Her eyes close as she tips her head back, filling the entire room around us.

The melody comes to a quiet end, and she whispers, "I'm so glad you're here."

"Me too."

"How long are you here for?" she asks, a slight quiver in her voice.

"Just the weekend," I say, resting my chin atop her head, feeling her shiver in response.

"Guess we have to make the most of it." Forcing her voice to stabilize, pulling out of my arms. "Let's get cleaned up, then hang out by the lake."

"Sounds so refreshing, I thought it was supposed to be cold in Wisconsin."

"It's July, it's hot everywhere."

"Fair, are you still at the B and B?"

"I actually rent the apartment upstairs now." Her statement comes out with her sounding shy, almost embarrassed, by the accomplishment of her apartment. But having a place of your own, whether renting or owning is an incredible accomplishment. It's something I have never known, and truthfully am not sure if I will ever know.

"That's amazing, Jules! Congrats, you've done amazing here. This place is beautiful, like you. I can tell you really pour yourself into your work. I'm booked at the B and B for the weekend." I grip her arms and try to chuckle at the change in my voice octaves as I try to show how excited I am for her.

"Why'd you book at the B and B?" She raises one eyebrow and scowls slightly.

"I didn't know what you had going on, and didn't want to make any assumptions."

"Oh," she replies, looking toward the floor.

"Do you want to stay together?" I ask by taking her hands.

She nods and whispers, "Yeah, I do."

"Okay." I nod.

"Okay." She nods again. "I'm going to clean up and grab some picnic stuff, I'll meet you at the B and B at six," she says after a few moments.

"Perfect, I probably smell after twenty-four hours of flying," I say.

She leans in close, taking a big breath in and almost instantly wrinkles her nose. "Maybe a smidge." She giggles, pinching her nose.

The action causes me to throw my head back and laugh.

"Get moving, pretty boy, I'll see you in a couple of hours," she says before planting a kiss on my cheek. I smile before grabbing my backpack and heading to the wooden door.

I'm pacing around the old wooden front porch of the bed and breakfast as the sun starts to dip lower and lower toward the horizon of the lake, when I see a silhouette of this beautiful woman in a sundress, carrying a picnic basket, and walking toward me. I thought I was nervous before, but holy smokes, Julie looks absolutely stunning. The pale pink sundress contrasts perfectly with her raven hair and the slight orange tint beginning to weave into the clouds.

"Jules, you look incredible," I say reaching out a hand for the basket as she approaches. I look town at my green pants and black T-shirt, different than the ones I had on earlier but also the exact same, and I start to wonder if I should maybe buy some new clothes.

"Come on. I have something I want to show you," she says, nudging my arm with a smile spreading across her face only meant for trouble.

I've never seen the lake during the day, or even when it wasn't covered in snow and ice, and I finally understand why everyone here loves the lake and gravitates to this park. It's beautiful. The setting sun paints golden streaks across the glassy still water. But even more beautiful is the pink reflecting off the shimmer of her glossy hair. I never thought I would see her again, let alone with the glow she has today, sun-kissed, wild, and free.

I jog slightly to catch up, slipping my hand into hers as we walk along the paved path throughout the park. The trees are combinations of deep forest and emerald green, and the grass looks lush and soft underneath our feet. The paved path begins to fade into a lightly worn dirt path, before disappearing altogether.

"Where are we going?" I ask as we walk farther into the park.

"You'll see in just a moment," she says, stepping in front of me, leading us through a dense brush to a small inlet clearing with a small private beach overlooking the sun setting behind the trees.

"This is amazing," I say, trying to take it all in. I don't ever want to leave. There are no people, no boats, you can only hear the sounds of the wind whispering, bugs buzzing, and birds chirping. I can't help but find joy and solace in the cooler, quieter air here.

"This is my spot. I don't think anyone else knows it's here." I turn to look at her and am stopped dead in my tracks. Julie is pulling the pale pink sundress up over her head revealing matching undergarment set.

She smirks as my eyes trace over her body, every curve, every muscle, every blemish.

"What are you doing?" I ask, though not able hide my smile.

"Going in," she says simply, as if it's nothing, before unstrapping her bra and letting it fall to the sand, sliding her hands to her panties next as she walks toward the water leaving a breadcrumb trail of clothes in her wake.

"You coming, or just gonna sit there and stare?" she says, looking over her shoulder.

I blink, let out a breath that sounds like half a laugh, and stand. "The view is too good not to stare."

She rolls her eyes before diving into the lake, coming up for air, her long hair slicked back, water dripping from the peaks of her breast. She turns, faces the lake and looks like a dream. Real, but just barely here, in front of me.

It takes a minute for my brain to finally catch up, her toned back, tan lines and sheer beauty, before I reach for my belt, not wanting to be away from her another minute. Pulling my shirt off, I can't help but feel the pressure of eyes sliding up and down my body. When I drop my shirt and look up, I see her eyes full of lust and hunger reaching out for me.

She stands, hands resting gently on her hips, looking pleased with herself before calling, "Your turn, pretty boy."

I laugh and shake my head before dropping my pants, sprinting to the lake, and diving in after her.

With the sun setting, the water becomes darker and darker making my next move easy as I stay beneath the surface to swim up on Julie. I plant my feet in front of her and slide my arms around her thighs before breaking the surface.

She shrieks, followed by her joyous giggle that I can't get enough of as I raise her into the air and slide her down against my body until we are face to face.

"I should've known you were holding out on me," I say, placing a gentle kiss on along her collarbone.

"Me? I have no idea what you're talking about," she says sarcastically, tilting her head back and arching into me.

I lean down to place another kiss along her neck before we stand foreheads together—silent, still.

Her entire body shivers as she says, "Come on, let's get some food and watch the stars." Then she turns to wade out of the lake.

And just like that, the stillness breaks. The lake, the woods, the sky are all still here, but the only thing I can really see is her.

In this moment I know I'd follow her anywhere.

15

I knew the weekend would go by fast. Too fast. What I didn't know was that it was going to hurt this bad leaving. Julie stayed at the bed and breakfast with me the first night, then I stayed at her apartment the rest of the trip.

The sun is barely rising behind the trees in the distance, giving the black sky hues of purple, orange, and pink, gently lighting the sidewalk from the door of her building to my car. Creek and Kettle is set to open in an hour, and I know she needs to get there and do her morning prep. What I didn't know is the amount of work that goes into making coffee and breakfast items for people, but it truly just makes me more amazed by Julie. Her work ethic, dedication, and drive are astonishing.

We got ready in silence this morning, eyes watery and fighting the demons in our minds.

Now she's standing by the door, early sunlight catching the raven hues of her hair, and I can feel the seconds slipping through my hands like sandy desert, I call home. Neither of us says anything. Afraid that one word, the word, makes everything real.

"Guess this is it," she says, voice soft but steady.

I nod, swallowing the lump that's been stuck in my throat. "Yeah. I guess so."

Everything I want to say is sitting in the humid air around us. I want to tell her that this has been the first real thing I've felt ever. That nothing in my life has ever felt this easy, that I have never laughed this genuinely, slept this well, or just lived like this before her.

But I don't. I can't. I can't make my mouth move to form the words.

And I know if I do, I won't be able to get in this car and drive away.

She forces a smile, but her eyes give her away, slowly glossing over with tears. "You'll write?"

"Of course, I'll write." My voice comes out rawer than intended. I was hoping to mask the break a little longer.

Her shoulders drop, just a little and my heart breaks further. I hate this, I hate the pain in her eyes, the words left unsaid and everything in between.

"Good. 'Cause I'll be waiting," she says, crossing her arms in front of her chest, as if giving herself a hug.

There's a long pause, long enough for the truth to hover between us, heavy and undeniable. I reach for her hand, just for a second, thumb brushing over her knuckles. It's nothing, really. But it feels like everything.

"I had the best weekend," I say quietly.

"Yeah," she breathes out. "Me too. Kind of wish it didn't have to end."

"Me too."

And that's all we let ourselves say. Anything more would tip us over the edge into something neither of us is ready to admit.

As I drive off, I glance between the blurring road and the rearview mirror. Julie stands where I left her, arms crossed against her chest, head hanging low, and I'm unable to see her face. Her raven hair gently bouncing around her head as she lets it all out.

This was the last thread attached to the string of my heart, and I find the tears silently streaming down my face next.

I know deep down in my heart, Julie is more than just my pen pal. She holds a piece of me, the missing puzzle piece. A piece I may never get back.

***

Back at base, Noah's waiting outside the residential tent for me, leaning against the pole of the entryway with that knowing look that makes me want to turn around and go anywhere else.

"Soooo," he says, dragging the word out. "Where'd you disappear to for leave this time? No one's seen you since Friday."

"Just...home," I say, tossing my duffel onto my cot, instantly recognizing my mistake. Noah knows, the only place I consider home is right here. Louisiana was a place I lived, but no part of me holds love for it.

He grins. "Home, huh? I thought you considered here home?"

I shake my head, accepting my defeat, knowing this will not end if I don't give him a real answer. "Met up with my pen pal."

Noah raises a brow. "*The* pen pal? The one who sends the good coffee? The one you won't tell us shit about?"

I shrug, trying to be nonchalant. "Yeah. That one."

He lets out a low whistle. "Man, you've been writing her for, what, four years now? You finally met her and vanished for a whole weekend? And your face is turning red and you're avoiding eye contact. Schmidty, do you have a girlfriend?"

Nine I correct in my brain. I did write her when we first were deployed, it just took four years to get consistent. I try to laugh it off, but my chest tightens. "There's nothing going on."

"Uh-huh." He smirks. "Right. And I'm Tom Brady."

I sink down on the edge of my bunk, running a hand over my face. The truth's sitting there, heavy in my chest. "It's different with her, you know? It's not like anything I've felt before. It's this quiet, but constant, deep ache I can't get rid of. But it's not a bad feeling, but it just...*is*."

Noah's grin softens into something more genuine. "Oh, bud," he says, clapping me on the shoulder. "You're down bad."

"I'm not." The words come too fast, too defensive.

He laughs, shaking his head. "Sure, man. Whatever you say. But I know the feeling. It's the same feeling I originally had with Ollie. The same feeling that I feel every day, and I can't escape. You're in love with your pen pal."

I look away, pretending to be busy with my gear, but the truth hums under my skin like a heartbeat.

Because I am.

And for the first time, I think I finally know what that means.

16

"Let's go," Kneland whisper-yells into the comms device as we start our two-mile trek back to the Humvee.

We walk in a silent straight line along the buildings of the desert city, while the city is still asleep. The mission went smoother than anyone dared to hope. We started in the middle of the night to keep the element of surprise in our favor. But now, the sky is starting to turn various shades of orange and pink as the hot, unforgiving sun threatens to crest over the horizon, and we need to get out of here immediately.

The early morning raid through a dense part of the city was relatively simple, truly a standard raid, for all intents and purposes. Get into the house, scope the surrounding buildings, take in anyone we found for questioning, and get out—all without making a sound. There were two people in the house when we raided, who were taken to a vehicle for a timely departure with about half our unit, while the rest of us remained to continue surveillance.

My least favorite type of "mission."

At least this time, I have Kneland and Gibson with me. Sanchez and Hayes aren't half bad either.

Our tight-knit unit of five is perfectly aligned, and we move as one through the dust-covered streets, hidden by the shadows, careful that the sand, dust, and gravel don't crackle under our boots.

Kneland walks point as always, scanning the intersections, alleyways, and rooftops for anyone out and about. He's followed closely by Gibson, who was responsible for signaling to the rest of us any information that needed to be communicated to us all. Sanchez and Hayes are the next two, and while they have real roles and responsibilities, they also bring some comedic relief. And then I'm bringing up the rear, looking for anything behind us.

"It's hotter than two goats in a pepper patch out here this morning," Sanchez says, sun starting to shine onto us.

The worst thing about the desert is the insane temperature changes. We left base in the middle of the night, when the air was cool, but by the time we get back each of us will want to strip to as little as possible and dump water over ourselves. The occasional cold shower is never a bad thing.

"I wish I could trade this gun for a fishing pole. Imagine fishing on the lake on a day like this," Hayes replies, closing his eyes and grinning as if he was deep into a daydream.

Kneland chuckles under his breath, followed by a long sigh, undoubtedly thinking of Fisher Creek and being home.

"Yeah, Hayes," Sanchez calls from behind him. "Except you'd probably scare all the fish away with your ugly ass."

More quiet chuckles throughout the group, even Gibson allows a half-smile to appear in the corner of his mouth. This is it. The best part about our job, when we're all here, intact, tired, but no injuries, no missing men, just here together as a family.

We round the final corner of town to where the Humvee is stationed, ready and waiting for our return. Corporal Tibbett is in the driver's seat, head on a swivel, watching for anything out of the ordinary. A faint smile appears on his face for no longer than two seconds when he sees us approaching, because god forbid he ruin his reputation as a hard ass.

We climb into the hot vehicle and check our surroundings one final time before making the trek back to base.

"Something's off," I finally say after fighting the gut feeling that has punched me square in the stomach.

"What?" Hayes replies.

"What's going on?" Gibson asks, looking at me.

"What do you see?" Kneland asks finally, turning around, looking toward me, frowning.

"Nothing," I said. "That's the problem."

They all look at me with blank stares.

"What do you mean?" Kneland asks, turning his body more toward me.

"The sun is starting to crest over the horizon, and there's no one out and about. Every other time we've been in the city, there are always people out, getting ready for the stands on the side of the road, or kids playing in the street before the heat boils us from the inside out. Nothing. We didn't see a single person. Doesn't that feel wrong?" I reply, scanning our surroundings again.

"Schmidty, there's nothing there," Hayes says, eyes tracking behind mine.

His eyes are incredibly well-trained; if there's something, he would see it.

"Hayes is right, Schmidt, he has the best eyes in the unit," Noah says, voice quieter, reassuring.

"I know, I know. Okay, let's just get the fuck out of here," I reply, unable to shake the feeling. But without any justifiable proof, what am I going to do? Just sit here? That is ridiculous.

It's an hour-long ride in the Humvee back to base, the sand dunes stretching the length of the horizon shaped into sharp peaks and smooths waves by the wind that never ends but never cools.

Off in the horizon, I can see the hazy shimmer of the heat radiating off the dunes, the light reflecting brighter and hotter the higher the sun raises. The only noise we can hear is the deep low growl of the engine, the crunch of the gravel under the tires, and the occasional growl of Sanchez's stomach because he refuses to pack a snack, ever.

"Does anyone have something we can feed this man?" I finally ask.

A quiet laughter sounds throughout the vehicle.

Sanchez replies hastily, "I can't help it. I'm hungry. I thought we'd be back by now."

"You always think we'll be back by now, Sanchez," Kneland chimes in from the front.

More laughter.

"Remind me to never be paired with you during hide-and-seek, your stomach will give us away," I say.

He glares at me, as I clap him on the shoulder, smiling. Hayes is practically on the floor laughing because everything is hilarious to him. And I take a minute to absorb our unit, the brotherhood, the friendships, the mentorship that we have with each other.

Gibson, the stern dad of the group who will always show up.

Kneland, the oldest, protector of the group.

Hayes, talented at everything, but constantly trying to fit in, even though we all love him.

Sanchez, the youngest and newest member of our family, who's the victim of the endless brotherly jokes and tricks.

And me, the one just happy to be here, have this family that I never had.

Pausing to look around the Humvee, we're all laughing and smiling, and I take a mental image of this. The life I dreamed for finally coming to fruition in front of me.

Then the first explosion hits.

The explosion isn't deafening, so much as gut-punching. The entire ground shakes ahead of us as the cloud of smoke begins to settle.

"It was ahead of us," Kneland says into the communication device. "We can't move forward on this path because…"

"Where there's one, there're usually more," I say into the device as the second explosion happens, this one behind us. The wave of heat and pressure pushes the vehicle forward, unsteadying our position.

"It's an ambush, we were set up!" Kneland yells through the comm device.

I move to the side of the vehicle to see if we have any leverage or vantage point from where we are, to fight our way out.

I'm just able to get the door open when the third and final explosion, the loudest one yet, goes off. The Humvee flips as I go flying out the open door.

Landing hard, the metallic taste of blood filling my mouth. My ears ringing with the high pitch piercing whistle that drowns out everything around me. The sand and dust coats my body, including my teeth adding an unbearable grittiness to my teeth. I can't move. I see the vehicle on its side, the dust kicked up around it, leaving grayish-tan smoke surrounding the area. My brain is screaming for my body to move but the blow to my head and neck must be too much, I don't even know if all of my limbs are still attached.

The ringing decreases, and I realize there is no gunfire, no shouting, just silence. I need to lift my head. I need to know if my entire unit is dead.

Where are they?

Do they know I'm out here?

The sharp electrical pain shooting from my neck down my spine followed by the immense feeling of nothing tells me that I'm royalty fucked.

Where the fuck are the others?

The air smells of burned rubber and fuel. This couldn't have been a random hit. It was methodical and placed. Planned.

And then it hits me.

It wasn't meant for us.

It was meant for the convoy that came back earlier. The one carrying the captive from last night's mission. That Humvee has been back at base for hours at this point. Their informant was either wrong, or the bomb waited.

Wrong vehicle. Wrong time.

I'm going to die, and this death isn't even meant for me.

I need to find the others, I need to see that Kneland and Gibson are alive. I want to hear one more joke from Sanchez and Hayes, and watch them fight like brothers back at camp.

I want more time with this family.

I hear something, something that sounds like a shout but my ears feel clogged and my brain fuzzy.

The last thing I see before everything begins fading is Noah, leaping from the vehicle and running toward me, a small streak of blood streaming down his face, and his mouth moving as he shouts something, but the words I can't hear. Everything is muffled and fading quickly.

I want to tell him about Julie, have him tell her I love her, tell him to fix things with Ollie, and that I love him. There are too many unsaid things, but the words don't form, my mouth doesn't move, and the tunnel vision begins to grow.

I know I'm not making it out of this alive, I can only hope that my unit, my brothers, my family, the only family I've ever had, make it back to base.

And so, the last thing I do is pray to the God I've never believed in that they survive, not just survive, but live. Truly live their lives to the fullest, because you never know when tomorrow might not happen.

And then…All I see is darkness.

17

EPILOGUE - NOAH

3 MONTHS LATER

"No," I reply, full of anger. "I can't take that, Commander Gibson."

"Son, he wrote this letter for you. You don't have to open it, but it's yours, so you'll take it and you will take time off," Commander Gibson says sternly. His face is scrunched with sorrow, worry, but also full of business. This is second nature to him. He has been in the army for over twenty-five years, he has lost many people.

I have lost many people over the years, my father, the love of my life, my best friend, and now, Jarred. But of those people, only two of them are dead. And one of them is my fault. I should have been there, more vigilant, more aware of our surroundings. I was in charge, it should've been me, not Jarred. Jarred didn't have a lot, but he did not deserve this.

"Thank you, sir," I say, fighting the anger and sorrow rising into my chest. I don't want to take time off, but these last three months have been a blur. I have been a shell of a human, barely scraping by each day. I'm a liability to my unit, but every time I close my eyes, all I see is Jarred falling, blood spilling from his body, and all I hear are the endless gunshots. And I'm drowning, drowning in the moment replaying over and over in my brain on an endless loop.

Commander Gibson places one hand on the small box, another on my forearm, a show of support or camaraderie, or whatever he is doing, and just nods.

"Take the next three months. Read the letter. Get the help you need—mandated or not. Then let's talk."

Now it's my turn to nod.

The desert around us is still, quiet, until the calm is interrupted by a low hum that begins to rumble, subtle at first, like a heartbeat growing faster and faster. The helicopter's rotors start to spin, slicing through the hot, dry air with rhythmic *whop-whop-whop* sound.

As the blades gain speed, the sound rising, filling the open landscape with a throbbing roar. Dust and grit lift in spirals, a mini tornado rising from the ground. The hum grows into a thunderous, chest-rattling vibration, more than just noise filling the air, a symbol indicating the beginning of the end. The start of the long journey back to civilization, ultimately ending in Fisher Creek. The middle-of-nowhere town with nothing to do but drown in my thoughts.

Metal creaks slightly under the strain, the engine growls with urgency, and the desert answers with a hollow echo.

Then, with a final surge, the helicopter lifts—blades shrieking against the wind, drowning everything else in its raw, mechanical fury.

Gibson's turning into a speck along the sand as we climb higher into the air.

It isn't until I can no longer see the shades of tan making up the desert sand, the tents, the entirety of the place I've called home for the last ten years, do I open Jarred's box. The box with his dog tags and a letter.

Normally, these letters are written to our loved ones, the ones who are the most important to us. Hell, I wrote mine to Mom and Bec, and then another to Ollie, not that I'll ever tell her that, or anyone else for that matter.

Jarred wrote his to me. I was the most important person in his life, and yet had the same likelihood he did of not making it. Except, somehow, there's this feeling deep inside me, that no matter the situation I would always be the one with Jarred. Jarred would've always been the one to go first. Simply due to his love and devotion for the army.

So I rip the end of the envelope, where the letter doesn't reach the end, and blow into it, creating space to pull out a small piece of lined paper folded into thirds.

Kneland,

If you're reading this, then you know what it means. That doesn't mean you get to blame yourself for this, for me. There is nothing you could have done to change the outcome.

I stop reading, my eyes blurring with tears. He's right, I do blame myself, and I don't know if I'll ever be able to change that feeling or rid myself of the guilt that I have for getting for going home. I get to live and he doesn't.

I sit in silence, with silent tears dripping down my cheeks, listening to the rotors spin, until I hear the pilot mention landing at the closest airport before starting the final trek back to Wisconsin.

There is something I need you to do. I need you to do it for me—but it's for you.

You have family, friends, people who love you and care about you, do not lose them.

You are my family, the only family I've ever had, really. Which means I know you, I know you haven't been truly happy since Olivia and you are hoping every letter, phone call is her. You are pushing everyone who loves you away.

I also know you are trying to deny this in your head, so stop.

I need you to get out. Retire. Go home. And find your happiness again.

I know what it's like to be unhappy and alone. That's not the life I want for my only brother.

Don't make me fight you in a bar when we meet again.

-Schmidty

18

Bonus Epilogue

Julie

Owning my coffee shop has been a blessing and a curse. I'm able to make a difference in my town's community, interact with the public, work alongside some of my favorite businesses, and make really delicious coffee. The part I didn't take into consideration, or particularly enjoy, is the back-end business work that needs to be done after closing each day. As I sit at my small oak desk that's set up in a literal broom closet in the back of the shop to go over the expense report, I start mindlessly scanning through the stack of mail that came today.

We were exceptionally busy when Linda, the postal worker, hobbled in to deliver my stack of bills, because what else would be delivered to the shop? It's June, so school's out and the teenagers are gathering wherever they can. I remember wishing we had a local place we could go to when I was in high school, which is a huge reason why I love this little shop, even if it's sometimes more work than anticipated.

But the shop was so busy, I threw the stack onto the desk and ran back out to help up front. We even ran out of cupcakes from the bakery in record time.

I need to make a note to order more cupcakes in the next order, I think, as I flip through the stack until I come across an envelope that's more yellow and tan than white, with crumpled dirt on the edges, and I instantly know who it's from.

Jarred.

My heart starts to race the same way it always does when I get one of these tattered envelopes. I know it's Jarred before even looking at the return label.

Jarred. The guy I spent only two weekends with, but just one night that changed my entire world. It's been almost ten years since I met him. The night I knew he would change my life forever. And every time I get one of these letters, my heart starts to skip a beat, I get a tingly sensation in my abdomen, and my hands get clammy.

I never used to believe in love at first sight. Don't get me wrong, I'm a romantic, and truly believe that true love, soulmates, and all of that is real. But to know immediately after meeting someone? That seems a little far-fetched. But the more Jarred and I have talk, the more I begin to doubt my own beliefs.

I rip the end of the envelope and dump the contents out onto the desk before unfolding the perfectly tri-folded piece of paper.

J,

I know you set one rule when we started this. This friendship. This relationship. Whatever we want to call this.

Don't fall in love with me.

I think about that night all the time, the one rule, and how I knew by the end there was no way I would be able to follow it. It's a good thing I've never really been good at following the rules, right? Cause we wouldn't be here, we wouldn't have this amazing friendship, which I didn't think was possible. Shh, don't tell Kneland. Don't get me wrong, I love Kneland, our friendship, and everything it has brought me in the world, mainly you. But there is something about you, Jules, that I just can't help but love. You are so kind, selfless, and exceptionally beautiful.

I would be lying if I said your letters weren't the highlight of my month and that I didn't spend every day waiting for the next one. You're my best friend, and if I have learned anything about my time in this desert, it's that you tell the ones you love that you love them because that time can be cut short in a split second.

And I love you, J.

I love everything about you. You've made a hopeful out of me. Hopeful the mail comes, hopeful the sun comes up, hopeful for the future. A future I have never thought I would get, need, or deserve, but now it's one where I see you and me together in that crazy little town you love.

I see a future; one I hope you will eventually see with me one day.

I know I'm breaking every rule we set, and it's okay if you don't feel the same way today or tomorrow, but know that, one day, I'll come back to Fisher Creek for you because I love you so much, Julie Rowe.

-J

A single tear starts to fall down the side of my reddened cheeks. I know I set the rules. I was afraid of the pain associated with loving a man on the other side of the world. But I didn't account for the agony that would accompany avoiding loving someone so important.

"I love you, too, Jarred. Always have," I say out loud, scattering the remainder of the mail on the side of the desk discarded for another day, and grab my pad, finally ready to tell Jarred.

"I see the future, too."

19

NOTE FROM THE AUTHOR

Don't worry, bookies! This is not the end of Julie Rowe's story. Stay tuned for book three of the Fisher Creek series, Sweet Ruin, where we will learn more about her. And I PROMISE it's not all sad. <3

20

SNEAK PEEK INTO BOOK 4 OF THE FISHER CREEK SERIES: SWEET RUIN

BEC KNELAND

The doorbell chimes as I walk through the heavy wooden door of Creek and Kettle for the third time today. Only this time, I'm met with quiet, no talking, no music, no one screaming into their phone or computer, just quiet. The first sense of peace I've seen in this building since it opened.

Julie is standing behind the counter, leaning against it with her elbows, overlooking a piece of paper. She looks up at the door chime with a brief smile as if she's expecting someone else to walk through the door. A look I see far too often that she refuses to talk about.

"Just me," I say, closing the door behind me as I head to the stool across from where she stands. She schools her face into a concentrated scowl before returning to the document in front of her.

"Damn, Julie, happy to see you, too," I say, assuming my position for our weekly meeting.

She glances up at me and looks exhausted. Her raven hair is tied in a messy bun with pieces falling down along her face; her entire body drooped in defeat. Her big brown eyes were full of apology.

"Sorry, Bec, today has been absolutely insane. We sold out of bakery items before ten and then again at noon."

"Shit. That's a new record. A good problem to have, but we definitely need to talk about partnership plans to remedy that. Where's your help? I didn't see Cass when I dropped more off at ten."

"Sick. She didn't make it today," Julie replies, completely slumping onto the counter at this point.

"You did this completely alone today?" I ask, amazed she's still standing on her feet. There had to be no less than fifteen people here at all hours open to close today. Heck, when I dropped more cupcakes, scones, and cinnamon buns off earlier, the line was out the door and halfway to my store already. No wonder she looks exhausted, and is caring for a toddler on top of it all. She's Superwoman.

Julie just groans in response, and I instantly know the answer is yes.

"Jesus, girl, have you eaten anything?"

"No," she replies, face flushing slightly, knowing I'm going to lecture her about taking care of herself.

"Go into that kitchen right now and pull out one of those sandwiches I know is in the fridge. This meeting can wait till you eat."

She peels—and I literally mean peels—herself off the counter before slowly sauntering into the back for something to eat. Julie is particular about who goes into the kitchen, so I'm better off waiting here.

I'm in this coffee shop every day, but never do I get to just sit down and take in my surroundings, truly enjoying my time here. Usually, I'm rushing in here to drop off her daily order and then running back to the bakery to get started on whatever's next. Today, it was gender reveal cupcakes for a couple visiting town with their family, and they want to surprise them.

To really sit here and look around, it's mesmerizing. Julie has really outdone herself. The wall behind the counter is exposed red brick, which is absolutely beautiful, and then has frames with hangings of local artists all across it. Each piece has a little tag underneath it with information regarding the artist and the cost to purchase.

I always hear Noah and Liv talking about how excited they were to leave our small town, the stress associated with everyone being deep into their business, and knowing their life but never truly understanding it. There is beauty and comfort in the day-to-day. Julie took that to the next level, fully embracing her small town and enhancing it tenfold by creating a community within it.

Before I even realize it, I'm walking to the edge of the counter, taking in each piece of art one at a time. The beautiful watercolor painting of the lake, bold abstract prints, moody rainy day film photography, and playful line sketches. Some are framed in sleek black, others hang on wooden clipboards or float freely on canvas, all blending into an incredibly curated storm.

I run my fingers along the ridges of the brick wall feeling each texture, absorbing the love put into this wall. Fingers continuing to grazing across each individual piece until I come across a small gold frame at the bottom of the wall, directly behind the register. I pause to look at the carefully crafted curves of the frame and realize it isn't an art piece, it's a handwritten letter.

A love letter.

J,

I know you set one rule when we started this. This friendship. This relationship. Whatever we want to call this.

Don't fall in love with me.

I think about that night all the time, the one rule, and how I knew by the end there was no way I would be able to follow it. It's a good thing I have never really been good at following the rules, right?

Holy shit. Julie has a love letter framed on her wall. The only frame that also doesn't have a price tag associated with it.

I feel a tickle in my insides as I continue to read the letter.

Cause we wouldn't be here, we wouldn't have this amazing friendship, which I didn't think was possible. Shh, don't tell Kneland. Don't get me wrong, I love Kneland, our friendship, and everything it has brought me in the world—mainly you. But there is something about you, Jules, that I just can't help but love. You are so kind, selfless, and exceptionally beautiful.

And then it hits me like a ton of bricks. Like a punch in the gut that knocks the wind out of me. Kneland. That's my last name. My brother's last name. There has to be another Kneland family in the world, right? But another Kneland, who brought Julie to someone?

That seems impossible.

The whoosh of the door swinging open pulls me out of my stupor, and I turn to see Julie walking toward me. She looks much more lively now that she has some sustenance in her body. Her head is held higher, she's moving quickly, and even has a smile on her face, and my heart breaks knowing I have to ask her about the letter.

The tension in the air is thick, heavy, unwavering.

"Hey, who wrote this letter?" I ask, trying to turn my voice gentle, quiet, and loving. She's one of my closest friends, a business partner, and someone I truly care about, but I also saw the shell of a human my brother was when he got home, and I need to know. Especially if someone else can share this loss with him.

My heart hurts, and there is a deep ache in my chest as I watch a piece of Julie crumble in front of me. Her eyes gloss over, and she inhales deeply, placing a hand on the counter next to her, as if steadying herself from falling over.

I feel like time has slowed as I turn and walk toward her, placing a gentle hand on top of hers.

"It was written by my first true love. His name was Jarred. Jarred Schmidt," she finally says through a shaky breath.

...To be Continued in Sweet Ruin...

21

ACKNOWLEDGEMENTS

Wow, guys, I truly did not think this novella was going to happen. Truthfully speaking, I didn't even realize Jarred and Julie had a story let alone a story together.

To Macayla and Leslie, thank you for asking for more of Jarred's story. Without you, this story would not exist and for that I am eternally grateful. But also thank you for the zoom calls, the texts, and knocking me off my ledge when things get tough.

Cause if you've written a book before, you know that there are a lot of tough moments.

Y'all are the greatest hype team there is.

Writing a book is a little like falling in love, messy, thrilling, full of plot twists, and only made possible by the people who stick with you through the chaos.

To my editor, Caroline, thank you for seeing the potential in this story and all of my stories. I appreciate your hard work, time, and commitment to not only myself but all of the other authors you work with. You are truly one of the kindest people I have met and have helped me in so many ways as I navigate this journey.

To my beta readers, thank you for reading early drafts, the unhinged comments, and the authentic reading reactions. I live for them and appreciate you getting me through this.

To my friends and family: thanks for pretending not to notice when I disappeared into fictional worlds and for loving me even when I spoke in plot points.

To every reader who picked up this book and gave these characters a chance, you are the heartbeat behind why I write. I hope this book made you smile, laugh, cry and fall in love with Jarred and Julie.

And finally, to love itself, it is messy, hard, but worth the risk.

Thank you, thank you, thank you.

I appreciate you all.

About the Author

Sierra Zinke is a romantic at heart who has the biggest soft spot for a good love story. She writes romance full of love, heat and emotion. Her books are full of big feelings, and feel like real life.

A northern girl at heart currently falling in love with the south as she lives in North Carolina with her other half and their two pups.

When she is not busy writing, she is a practicing chiropractor in North Carolina, striving to help people continue their favorite activities. Otherwise she truly loves reading, sports, and trying new restaurants.

You can check out her books at www.zinkewrites.com and say hi on social media @zinkewrites!!!

48976CB00028B/2493